WALLACE, THE WANDERING PIG

Wallace,
the Wandering Pig

Judy Van der Veer

Illustrated by Paul Galdone

Harcourt, Brace & World, Inc., New York

WALLACE, THE WANDERING PIG

Chapter One

T HE polka-dot pig was born in a very clean place, in the farrowing house in a farrowing pen. Scientifically it was perfect. Clinically it was pure. The farrowing house was like a pig factory in which litter after litter of piglets were manufactured. They came into being excited and squealing and surprisingly strong, and very soon they hurried to find their mother's milk.

This polka-dot piglet looked like his ten brothers and sisters, with ears that hung forward to make roofs over his eyes. He was silvery colored with soft dark dots all over him. He had a tightly curled tail, and he was a beautiful little pig, round and soft.

Soon after he realized he was alive, he was playing with his sisters and brothers, all tumbling around and biting like puppies and chasing one another about in the small pen. He liked sleeping in a warm place, either in a pile of his littermates or on the soft, warm side of his reclining mother.

Like the others, he was very fond of his mother's milk, and before he was very old, he enjoyed helping his mother eat her mash. Food was very important in the life of the polka-dot pig.

Before he was three months old, a terrible thing happened. A hired man took all the piglets away from their mother and put them into what was called the weaning house. They, with a number of other piglets from other litters, were well fed, and they had a roof over their heads, though the sides of the house were open to let in fresh air and slanting bars of sunshine. At first they all complained, wanting milk, but in a few days they began to forget about their mothers and the warm milk.

The next step would have been promotion to what was called the growing pen, and after that the fattening pen. But something happened to change the routine. The hired man decided to turn the weanlings out into pasture, where there was grass, shade, and a pond.

At first the little pigs were delighted with the fresh spring grass, but after a while the sun beat hotly on their backs, they began to burn, and they grew thirsty. Being smart little pigs, they headed for where they had last had water, which was the weaning pen.

But they couldn't get there. Instead, they came across a woven wire fence, which held them back, and desperately, squealing and unhappy, they became a squirming pile of hot, thirsty little pigs, the under ones unable to breathe good air.

The polka-dot pig knew, right away, that this was a very bad situation and fought to free himself of the tangle of other pigs, to make his way through the fence that was trying to keep him from his familiar quarters. He kicked, pushed, rooted, squirmed, shrieked. He managed to squeeze through a small hole he made, and grunting happily to himself, he trotted briskly in the direction of the weaning house and water.

The hired man saw him and gave chase. This confused the polka-dot pig so much that, darting this way and that, he ran off course and ended up by hiding on a brushy hill behind the ranch house. The hired man couldn't find him. Then he heard the loud squealings of the piglets against the fence, saw that others were escaping through the hole that the polka-dot pig had made, and hurried to tend to matters there.

The polka-dot pig hadn't in the least liked being chased. It had frightened him badly, and he started off up over the hill. He wasn't happy in his freedom. His back was red and sore from the unaccustomed direct sunshine. He was hot and thirsty, and he really didn't know which way to go. But he wanted to get away from the frightening place where he had been chased by the man.

There was some moisture in the green grass he ate, and once he drank up a small puddle left from the last rain. He wallowed in the leftover mud, which made his sunburn feel better at first but soon made it feel worse.

He slept for a while in the shade of a scrub oak and wakened to keep wandering. When night came, he rooted a bed for himself in the soft earth.

He didn't sleep well. He heard coyotes howling and owls hooting, and he shivered with the night air touching his sunburn.

Chapter Two

Aᴇᴛᴇʀ two days of roaming about, the polka-dot pig began to grow thin, and his backbone was an uncomfortable ridge. His eyes grew sore from the unaccustomed sunshine, and his tail lost its curl and drooped miserably. He was an unhappy and lonesome little pig, but restlessly he kept traveling, as if he felt that in time he would arrive at some good place.

He talked to himself a great deal, as pigs do, making comments about everything he saw. When he saw a coyote watching him, he made a blasting, whistling sound of alarm and ran. This sprint took him over the hilltop and started him down the other side. He would have liked to see others of his kind, have sweet rich grain to eat and lots of water to drink.

Most pigs, no matter how young, once strayed, will find their way home again, but this pig had been too frightened and confused when he left. Now it seemed to be his idea to find another, better home.

On the fourth day, before the sun was up, he found it. He saw a barn, smelled grain and hay, and hurried down the last slope, making joyful remarks to himself. His tail, which had hung so limply with despair, now kinked into a hopeful curl, and his ears flopped with the motion of his going.

The delicious smells grew stronger as he reached the corral by the barn, and he sniffed hopefully by the barn door and found grains of oats that had fallen and small leaves of alfalfa hay. But it wasn't enough. His eager nose discovered all there was. Soon it was inside him, and he wandered around the barn. He smelled water, but the watering trough was too tall, and stretch as he might, his snout could not reach a drink. His tail hung dejectedly again.

A big, warm, milky-smelling cow watched him and couldn't decide what he was.

The sun was just coming up when Molly Ames, milk bucket on arm, headed for the barn with her black-and-white shepherd dog Lucy walking beside her.

As she approached the corral, Molly saw that the cow, whose name was Bossy, was intently watching some animal, her eyes and ears alert. Molly hurried to see what it was. But she couldn't get a close look. The polka-dot pig, startled, made a wild, blasting sound and ran. He hid in the brush before Molly could see more than a blur. Lucy was not far behind him.

"Lucy, come back," Molly called, and tried to see what the dog was after. "It did look like a pig," she thought, "but where would a pig come from?"

Lucy, obedient, returned, and Molly looked at the pig's tracks in the soft earth. "It must be a pig, but how strange . . ."

She looked around but saw no further signs and decided to milk Bossy now and search later. Bossy's calf was already demanding its share of the milk.

That morning, as it happened, the calf got more milk than usual because, when she was halfway through milking, Molly stopped and hurriedly hung the bucket on a peg in the barn.

Lucy had been unable to resist following the animal she had seen. She had found him, and when Molly had looked up, she saw the shepherd dog shouldering the squealing pig along, bringing him toward the corral.

With Lucy's help it was no trouble to catch the pig, who was tired anyway. He was a large armful, and he squealed with fresh enthusiasm. "Why you poor little thing," Molly said softly, noticing his high backbone, his thinness, and his brightly burned skin. "Poor piggy."

Her voice did it. The squeals stopped. The polka-dot pig nestled happily into kind arms. Molly carried him into the barn and put him down in a big, empty horse manger. She gave him some grain and hay and poured the cat's saucer full of new milk, which the pig thirstily turned to first of all. Eager as he was, he drank carefully, not spilling a drop. Molly brought him water, and as he drank, his tail suddenly resumed a jaunty tightness, which made Molly laugh. "Already you're happy to be my pig!"

She watched until she thought he had eaten enough, and after she had taken the milk to the kitchen, she returned for him. She put him down on the kitchen floor. He stayed close to her feet as she strained the milk and washed the breakfast dishes. "Wonk," he said, and added, "Ernk."

Lucy, who had a shepherd instinct equally mixed with maternal feeling, began washing him with her warm, moist tongue. The polka-dot pig felt among friends with this dog and this human. He made a few playful bounces across the kitchen floor.

As soon as she had finished the kitchen work, Molly took him on her lap and gently washed his eyes, which had grown sore and mattery. Then she rubbed oil into his sunburn and

told Lucy not to lick him any more. The pig, released, found a square of sunshine on the floor. Molly put down a towel, and he went to sleep in a warm, soft place.

He must have dreamed, for he grunted in his sleep and his tail jerked.

"What a sweet pig," Molly thought, "a polka-dot pig. What will I name him? He's so long and lean."

Finally she decided to name him Wallace, after the best cowboy on the ranch, who was also long and lean.

When Molly's husband Bert and the cowboy Wallace came in to eat at noon, it would have been difficult to say who was the more amazed to see a pig in Molly's kitchen.

"What is *that*?" demanded Bert. "Where did it come from?"

"You ought to be able to see what it is," Molly told him. "It's a pig. But I haven't the faintest idea where he came from."

"Sorriest-looking pig I ever saw," Wallace observed. "He's got red ears."

"That's sunburn," Molly explained, "but soon he'll be beautiful. Wait and see. Anyway, don't make fun of him. I named him after you."

"Oh," said Wallace, not knowing whether to be pleased or not, and handed Wallace the pig a piece of his bread and butter. Wallace made a glad grunt and gobbled it. "Cute little feller, ain't he?" the cowboy decided.

"But you can't keep a pig in the house," Bert protested.

"He's got to stay inside for now because of his sunburn. And a pig, you know, is a very clean animal. Pigs don't like the way some people keep them in dirty pens. I haven't had a pet pig since I was a little girl," Molly added wistfully. "I had a runt I raised on a bottle, and she loved me and followed me everywhere."

"Pigs are smart all right, but, honey, why don't you keep him in the barn until his sunburn is better?"

"The barn's too far from the house, and he's lonesome."

Bert grinned at her. "All right. We don't need a pig, but we have one. I don't see how you can keep him forever. After all, a pig is for pork. And when he's out, he'll get into your garden and root up everything and be an awful bother in a lot of ways."

"No he won't. The garden has a good fence to keep the chickens out, anyway."

"Pigs kill chickens," Wallace the cowboy stated.

"Not always. Only when a pig is in a pen and bored and hungry and a chicken flies in. This Wallace won't kill my hens."

"No use arguing with her," Bert said. "Just wait until the pig gets big and damages everything, and she'll be glad to part with him. A *little* pet pig is cute, but a big one is for bacon."

Molly protested. "You keep saying things like that. There's no reason why a meat animal can't be a pet and a friend, except that people aren't in the habit of thinking of them in this way. Why can't I keep him as long as I can?"

"Sure," said Wallace the cowboy, "he's my namesake."

Bert had to grin again. "I don't care, honey. Sooner or later we'll probably have to get rid of him, so don't get too attached to him." And he hugged his young wife, whom he loved very much. "Come on, Wallace, we got to finish that fence this afternoon."

Molly sighed with relief after they were gone. She knew

that her husband wasn't really glad to have the pig, but he wasn't going to object strenuously, and she was going to be able to enjoy her pet.

As for the pig, there had never been any doubt in his mind. He'd found a home he liked.

Chapter Three

As Molly had predicted, before many days Wallace was a different-looking pig. His sunburn healed and his skin softened and became comfortable again, he put on weight, and his pretty hazel eyes grew bright and clear. His silvery coat, decorated with soft dark dots, glistened in the sunshine.

More spring rains came. The land was damp and sweet, and Molly enjoyed the sight of her pig rooting in the delicious earth. As he dug about, the pig made soft crooning sounds to himself, partaking of the crumbling soil in a way that no human could.

Lucy, the dog, continued to be his friend, and they stayed together. When Lucy heard a ground squirrel chatter and took off after it, the pig scampered behind her. Sometimes, overcome with joy, Wallace squealed a little song and went bouncing around in a funny pig dance.

He went with Molly and Lucy to the barn every morning and had his breakfast of hay and grain while Molly milked. One morning he finished his breakfast before Molly had finished milking, and then he hurried to the cow and wanted to dip his snout into the milk bucket, which was disturbing to both Molly and the cow.

Molly stood up, hung the bucket in a safe place, and tied a rope tightly around Wallace's neck. A pig is really not well constructed to be tied by the neck, but Molly knew that a young one can be trained to be tied that way and grow used to it.

Wallace expressed displeasure loudly, and when Molly attached the other end of the rope to a fence post, his screams must have been heard miles away. He pulled and stamped his feet and bounced about, and finally, unable to pull free, he lay down with his front hoofs before him and regarded Molly and the cow sadly.

As soon as she finished milking, Molly untied the rope from the fence post and gave Wallace a lesson in how to be led. Since he was glad to go anywhere that Molly went, he soon learned to yield to the tug of the rope, and heeled like a good little dog.

After that Molly tied him every morning for practice and served him his breakfast while he was tied. The rest of the day he was free to wander where he liked, and sometimes Molly let him come into the house. She didn't allow him in

the house when Bert was there because she knew that Bert
didn't care to have a pig in the house, and there was no use
annoying a good husband like Bert.

The men started the spring gathering of the cattle so that
the calves could be branded and earmarked and vaccinated
against various ailments, and all of them had to be sprayed
for ticks. On a morning when there were bright white clouds
moving on a deep blue sky, causing shadows to wander over
hills, Molly couldn't stay in the house. She knew where the
men would be working that day, in a valley not distant,
where there was a corral and a squeeze chute.

She saddled her horse Ranger, and Lucy came along, eager
to run after the horse, and Wallace came bouncing along
with Lucy. "Oh dear," Molly thought, "the pig shouldn't
go." She considered tying him, but she didn't like to leave
him tied when no one was around to keep an eye on him. She
got on Ranger and took off at a brisk gallop, planning to
leave the pig behind. She didn't think that Wallace would
run very fast for very long.

But he did. She glanced back to see him hurrying along
not far behind Lucy, and finally she brought Ranger to a

walk. "I guess it won't hurt him," she decided. "It's cool today." An overheated pig could become very sick, but today, if she didn't ride fast, it wasn't likely that he'd get too hot. It was, in fact, fun to have a pig along with the dog, especially this polka-dot pig who enjoyed everything so much. The land was still bright and fragrant with grass and wild flowers, and Wallace sampled everything, so that he appeared to be eating a salad along the way.

The range cows seemed to know that there was going to be a bad time for themselves and their calves in a corral, and at gathering time they wanted to stay up in the hills in the thick brush. Bert, Wallace, and two Indian cowboys had had some hard riding, working cows and calves out of the chaparral and down into the valley. Swift and well reined as their quarter horses were, they couldn't do well when the cows were in dense thickets, and there was much yelling, swinging of ropes, and wild riding where footing was unsure.

Even when the cattle were finally down in the small level valley, they wouldn't give up. From time to time some wise animal would break away. A cow can run like the wind, and there was hard riding and loud cussing before the bunch got to the corral gate.

Just at the moment when all should go well, just as the animals were nearly corralled, there was a sudden and fast stampede. At the wrong second Lucy heard a squirrel and, with the pig at her heels, ran toward the sound, which was near the corral.

The pig was too much for the cows' nerves. No one was expecting such a sudden disaster, but almost at once five riders were racing to head off the cows. The odd thing was that while no pig was to be seen, there were loud pig sounds coming from down among tail ends and hoofs. Most of the cows escaped to the brush again. One little bunch, about a dozen, got corralled, and with them was Wallace the pig.

Bert didn't say a word. He took down his rope and after several tries, for the pig was too much among legs, managed to make a neat catch and started dragging the squealing pig from the corral. This unnerved his horse, who was used to roping and holding nearly anything but a noisy pig. He started to pitch. Bert lost his hat and was hard put to keep his horse under him reasonably well. He made a bad ride, but he stayed on, and not wanting to get tangled, he let his rope slip from around his saddle horn, and Wallace was free, dragging the rope.

Molly leaped from Ranger, dropping the reins on the ground so that he would stand. She crept under the fence, seized the rope, dragged Wallace out, removed the rope, got on her horse, called Lucy and Wallace, and rode away from there as if she were escaping from a nest of hornets, which, in a way, she was.

The men were furious. It meant a day's extra riding to gather the cattle from the brush again, and the cows forever more were going to hate going through that corral gate.

Molly expected to hear a lecture when Bert got home that night, but he didn't say a word. He didn't say a word about the pig, but he didn't say a word about anything else, either, and, in a way, that was even worse.

Chapter Four

After that, on days not too warm, Molly took short rides because it was fun to have Wallace along. Sometimes he stopped for several minutes, eating and rooting about, then, discovering that he was left behind, said "Woosh!" and galloped with ears flapping gaily. He huffed and puffed as he caught up.

One day when Molly was inside the house, she heard such happy pig conversation that she went outside to look. Wallace had broken part of the fence and was demolishing her flower garden. She found a rope and tied him up for punishment, though of course she knew that he did not comprehend why he was tied.

Molly sighed and went to work on the fence. The next day Wallace found a new place to break through. Unhappily, for she felt tired, Molly began the project of rebuilding and reinforcing the whole garden fence. Wallace had many acres in which to root around, and he could very well stay out of the flowers.

One morning she overslept, and when she arrived late at the barn, Wallace and Bossy were inside enjoying hay and grain. The pig had worked the door open for his own benefit, and the cow had benefited also. She had her nose in a sack of grain and had already eaten too much for her health.

Molly chased the animals out, looked sadly at the broken

door, and to her horror saw Bossy lie down and begin to bloat. She ran and called Bert, who was working on a nearby fence, and he came to stare at the cow in dismay.

"I hope she didn't get a drink," he said.

"No, she came right out and went down. She's bloating fast."

Bert glanced inside the feed room and whistled. Wallace had torn open sacks of grain and scattered it all about. But he had known better than to overeat, and only the cow was sick.

"A horse or cow could die because of that pig getting the door open," Bert said.

"I know. Here, help me tail up Bossy."

It wasn't difficult to get the cow up because she hadn't been down long, and she hadn't eaten as much as she might have had Molly not come when she did. They kept Bossy moving, around and around the corral, and before long she began to feel better and the bloat went down.

Uncheerfully Bert started repairing the barn door.

A few days later he said, "I ought to take time and build a strong pen for that pig."

"I hate to see Wallace in a pen. He really wouldn't be much fun, and he wouldn't have much fun, either."

"But I don't see any point in all this. You've been struggling with the garden fence, and he gets in, and he could get in the barn again. I have an idea of what to do with him that wouldn't be bad."

Molly looked thoughtful. "Ordinarily I wouldn't hear of it, because I dearly love my pig. But if we could find a good home for him . . . well, maybe. You see, I'm planning to get a new pet."

"Oh, no!" Bert groaned. "What next?"

23

Molly smiled mysteriously. "You can be part owner, and you'll like it. It'll keep us both busy, though. In some ways it will be quite different from Wallace. It'll have two legs, I hope . . ."

"What? Oh, Molly! You mean?"

"I mean we're going to have a real human baby, I'm pretty sure."

"Molly, Molly! I hope it will be a girl exactly like you!"

"And I want a boy just like you!"

Bert was suddenly so happy that he forgot what he was going to say on the subject of getting rid of Wallace. A few days later he thought of it again.

"Molly, about that pig. Now this is a cow ranch, and a pig doesn't fit. You've seen what trouble he can cause. This really isn't the place for him, and I'm worried. Without meaning to, when he's bigger, and he's growing fast, he could knock you down and hurt you. It's all too dangerous now that we've got to think about our baby."

Molly looked up from her sewing. She was trying to learn to make baby clothes. "What good solution do you have to offer?"

Bert's face lit up with enthusiasm. "A dandy! There's going to be that children's fair, you know, down in town. And they need a pig this size for the greased-pig contest."

"Greased-pig contest?"

"Yes, you know. They grease up the pig and make him slippery and turn him loose for the kids to catch, and the one who captures him gets to keep him. And it's all for a good cause. Money for the kids' farm club."

Molly was stricken. "How dreadful! Poor little Wallace would be terrified with a pack of screaming kids chasing him."

"Naw. It wouldn't hurt him a bit. He'd have fun giving the kids a bad time catching him."

"It isn't fun for any animal to be frightened. I think it's terrible."

"Aw Molly. You're all wrong. It wouldn't bother him at all, and the kid that won him would be tickled to death and give him a wonderful home. They've always had greased-pig contests. Nothing wrong with it."

Molly reflected that any often-repeated event becomes customary, and people accept it. She realized that Bert was like a number of good people, not intentionally cruel but seeming to condone what she and a few others might consider cruel. Bert wouldn't permit anything that he thought was really wrong.

She sighed. "I don't approve. But I don't know what to do. You won't be happy if I keep Wallace, I know."

"If the pig hadn't happened to wander here," Bert reasoned "somebody would have killed him by now. You gave him a second chance, and the kid that wins him will give him a third chance."

"Maybe," said Molly doubtfully. "Who knows?"

Chapter Five

Bᴇʀᴛ built a strong crate, coaxed Wallace into it with a can of grain, and nailed everything together firmly. Wallace the cowboy helped him to lift the crateful of pig to the back of the pickup.

Molly stayed mournfully out of sight. She couldn't even bear to pat Wallace good-by. She hoped that whatever child captured him would learn how Wallace loved to stretch out and have his belly rubbed, how he enjoyed to have the soft place behind his ears tickled.

Inside his crate Wallace shrieked with dismay, pushed, rooted, tore with his teeth. He couldn't get out. It was only a short trip to the little country town, but Wallace didn't enjoy a moment of it. He didn't like the winding road; he didn't like the wind that whistled through the bars of his crate. In spite of the fresh air, he felt carsick.

He didn't like it any better when they reached town. His crate was placed under a shade tree at the edge of the fair grounds, and it was a noisy place. Wallace didn't understand what made all the different noises, but they were frightening.

Then children came and laughed at him and poked at him with sticks. He cowered and screamed for help, but Molly didn't hear him. No one saw his misery. He was only a funny pig who squealed.

Some men looked at him and said, "He'll dress out nicely. Hey, you kids, stop pestering him for a while. He'll get wore down so's he can't run fast."

No kind voice spoke to him at all. He couldn't understand anything, and he quaked with terror.

A tall, thin girl wandered along and stared at him. She had straight light brown hair cut below her ears and a fringe of even bangs above warm brown eyes. Like the others she wore blue jeans and a plaid cotton shirt. But unlike the others she looked at the pig with compassion. She sensed his terrible dismay.

She was eleven years old, and her name was Christina Wood. She didn't know why she was usually the only one who would say of some distressed animal, "Poor thing." Other people never seemed to notice, or else had trained themselves not to care. Perhaps, she thought hopefully, when she grew older, she would learn not to care so much, not to suffer for every suffering animal.

Her mother was always talking about how she would outgrow different things, such as her tendency to be shy of people or her feeling of awkwardness because just now she was tall for her age. She sighed and wondered if she really wanted to outgrow her feeling of being sorry for animals. She supposed that it was good that some people were made that way. But it was difficult when you were that kind of person, because you were always being hurt.

She looked sadly at Wallace and thought that this was the poor pig that was going to be chased all over the place and scared out of its wits. It was a game she wouldn't enter, a thing she didn't even want to see.

Over the loudspeaker she heard the announcer talking about the next event, the greased-pig contest. "Some kid will

27

win a good porker, a chance to provide his family with some mighty good eating. Come on, kids! This is gonna be fun."

"Oh," thought Christina, "some horrid boy will win him and keep him in a dirty pen and never be nice to him at all. . . ." She started to walk away as two men came and picked up the crate and carried it toward the show ring.

Immediately Christina became engulfed in a crowd of people that shoved toward the ring, and without wanting to, she found herself about to be a spectator of the greased-pig event.

Wallace's crate was put down in the center of the ring. A claw hammer pulled some boards loose above his head. Big hands came at him. Shrieking, Wallace drew back. But in his crate he couldn't escape the hands that covered him with oily black grease. Another board was removed, the men stepped back, and Wallace scrambled out. He stood still, too horrified to move, staring at noisy enemies everywhere.

"All right, kids, go get him!"

Completely panicked, Wallace screamed, ran, dodged. A mob of howling children pursued him, fell over each other, grabbed at his ears, his tail, his legs. One boy cast himself upon him and almost had him, but being slippery, Wallace escaped. Other children tumbled over the prone boy.

Christina, her heart going as fast as the terrified pig's, felt his fear as her own. Suddenly she forgot everything else and went after him, her long legs flying. She had a slight advantage that no one noticed—while other children had been running at top speed, she had been standing still. The spectators were too busy roaring with joy to observe that she had made a late entry.

Suddenly Christina paused, reached down, and rubbed her

hands in the dirt, thinking that if ever she caught the pig, the dirt on her hands would make him less slippery. Now children and pig were at the far end of the arena. She was nowhere near, but if the pig could escape them this time, he'd have to run her way. She would step aside enough so that he wouldn't run back, and this would be her one chance to grab him.

"It won't work," she thought desperately, "but it's got to!" It should be to her advantage that the pig was growing exhausted, but then a big boy grabbed him by one hind leg as he raced down the stretch.

The crowd yelled louder as it looked as though the pig were captured for sure, but his fear gave him the strength for a last breathless struggle, and the grease made the boy's hand slip.

Christina flung herself on him, one arm around his neck holding him back, one arm gripping a front ankle. What weight she possessed was upon him, and determinedly she hung on and on as the pig screamed as only a pig in distress can scream. The people all cheered, but Christina couldn't hear them.

"Poor Piggy," she panted as she hung on, and the contest was over. Two men rushed to help her. They got the pig stuffed into his crate and the boards nailed down.

Everyone but Christina was laughing. Wallace, quaking and fighting to breathe, was grateful to be in his crate. It was better than out there.

The men carried the crate back to the tree, and Christina sat down beside it and began talking softly, trying to comfort her pig.

Chapter Six

HER parents came along just then and regarded Christina with amusement. "Why in the world did you have to catch that pig?" her mother wanted to know.

Her father was laughing. "You didn't really want to come here today. We had to talk you into it, and look what happened!"

"You who never want to enter into any games, and you ran right in and snatched that pig. I can't believe it." Her mother turned to her father. "Now what will we do?"

Mr. Wood said, "You don't really want a pig. Tell you what—we'll find someone right here who'll buy him, and we won't have to take him home."

"But I *want* to take him home. He's mine. He's my pig. I rescued him."

"But a pig! You can't keep a pig forever. And you wouldn't want to eat him. Be sensible. Wouldn't it be fun to sell him now and have some money?"

"No. No, it wouldn't. This pig is my very, very own."

Other people gathered around and found this discussion entertaining. Christina's parents were embarrassed. Christina was about to cry with nervousness. She was an uncomfortably intense child. Rather than be involved in an argument with his daughter publicly, Christina's father grinned, rather sheepishly, and gave in for the moment.

31

"All right, we'll take him home. But you can't keep him the rest of his life. You'll see. Guess I'll have to borrow a pickup from somebody to haul him home."

Christina brightened. Once she got her pig safely home, she could manage to keep him. Her father went off to look for a friend who had a truck, and she continued to talk kindly to Wallace, who was too engrossed in his own personal nightmare to pay attention.

Christina's mother stood around helplessly and kept saying, "But, darling, really . . ."

Finally Mr. Wood returned with his friend, Bob Peerling. The men picked up the crate, and Wallace was placed in a pickup truck. Christina scrambled up and crouched by the crate to offer what comfort she could.

When they reached the ranch house where Christina lived, Bob stopped and stuck his head out of the cab. "Where do you want him unloaded?"

"We'll put him in the pony's box stall in the barn," Christina decided. "Drive over there. The pony's out in pasture."

Evidently her parents had stopped to talk to someone. They weren't home yet. Christina helped carry the crate into the barn and closed the stall door firmly. "Now," said Bob, "I'll pry a few boards loose so he can get out, and you two start getting acquainted. Probably he'll be a nice pig when you get him cleaned up."

"I'm as dirty as he," Christina said, suddenly noticing the sad state of her best plaid shirt.

Bob got boards loose, but this time Wallace was in no hurry to leave his refuge.

"You'll both do all right," Bob promised. "I've got to get back."

Christina remembered to thank him before she started

further discussion with her pig. "Poor little fellow, don't worry. I'll be good to you."

Wallace began to realize that life was improving. He stuck out his head and looked at the source of this kind voice. Then, cautiously, he crept out and stood in clean straw and softly said, "Erful."

"But it isn't erful; it's nice," Christina told him delightedly, and held out her hand. Trustingly Wallace nosed it.

"How funny!" Christina said. "Two even little round holes in a round snout. And soft, too."

She would have liked to pet him more, but he was too covered with grease and dirt. Finally he sat down as a dog sits and looked at her with what Christina was sure was a pleased expression.

"Probably he's hungry and thirsty," she decided, and went away and left him alone. Uneasily he poked at the door. But soon she returned with water in a bucket, and after he drank, she went away again and hurried back with hay and grain.

He wasted no time enjoying the good food, grunting to himself as he ate, and now his tail tightened into a curl.

She left him again, and this time was gone longer. When she returned, she carried a bucket of warm soapy water, a scrub brush, and one of her mother's best bath towels.

"You'll like this," she told him, and he did. There is nothing that a pig enjoys more than a good bath. As she scrubbed his back, he made little sounds of pleasure. She was careful not to scrub too hard on his sensitive ears, and she didn't get a bit of soap into his eyes. Face and chin got polished, and then she reached under to start on his belly. Wallace promptly lay down and stretched out to enjoy this all the more.

When finally he was clean—Christina had had to make extra trips to the house for fresh buckets of soap suds and rinse water—she rubbed him briskly with the towel while he crooned with joy.

He was a sparkling pig, silvery and splashed with dark dots. Even his little cloven hoofs were shining clean. She thought about how small those hoofs must have been when he was a new piglet and how a little pig steps on pointed hoofs. "Like a ballet dancer," she thought.

She asked, "Shall I name you Polka Dot?" and wondered if he had had a name before. "I must teach you to lead so that I can take you walking," and she got her pony's lead rope and tied it about his neck.

This was old stuff for Wallace, but Christina didn't know it, and she thought that he was very bright to learn so quickly how to lead.

After she circled the stall with him a time or two, she opened the door and took him outside. He pattered along close by her feet, and she led him from the barn to the house. Just then her parents came driving in. Christina was sure that she and the pig must be making a very good impression. "Isn't he sweet?" she asked with pride.

"He certainly is clean and docile," her mother said, "but, darling, look at yourself!"

Christina had to put Wallace back in the barn and go take a bath before she could continue making friends with him.

Chapter Seven

T HAT night at supper, Christina could talk of nothing but her pig. "I wonder where he came from. I wonder if he had a name."

"Bert Ames donated him, I think," her father said. "Why don't you phone the Ameses and ask about him?"

"Oh, I didn't know that," Christina's mother said. "Then that must be the pig Molly Ames had. You know Molly, don't you Christina?"

"I don't think I remember her."

"Yes, you've seen me talk to her when we met in the store or somewhere. A pretty, red-cheeked young woman. A pleasant sort of person."

Christina was up and looked in the phone book. "Finish eating first," her mother suggested, "and don't phone the Ameses right at mealtime."

"If she's so nice, I wonder why she gave up her pig. She couldn't have loved him very much to let him be chased by all those kids." Christina sighed and sat down again. "Mama, why don't you phone Mrs. Ames?"

"Oh, don't be shy. That's silly. Just phone her and tell her that you won the pig and find out what his name is. I'm sure she'll be glad to know that you have him."

"But not for long," her father said.

"Oh, Daddy! He's my own pig!"

"How are we going to keep a pig?"

"I'll make him a pen. Alberto will help me."

Alberto was the Mexican who worked on the ranch. Christina's father raised and sold quarter horses and said that he couldn't run the place without Alberto. Alberto was growing old, but he knew a great deal about horses, and he was a good, steady worker. He also was a very good friend of Christina's.

"Alberto has other things to do," her father reminded her.

"He'll find time to help me," Christina said with assurance. "Now, please, may I phone Mrs. Ames?"

Molly answered the phone. Christina said, "Mrs. Ames? This is Christina Wood, and I caught the pig you used to have and I just love him."

"Oh!" said Molly. "This is too good to be true. I am so glad. I was terribly worried. He is the *best* little pig."

"Oh, I know. And you ought to see him. I gave him a bath, and he's beautiful. He likes me. Did you have a name for him?"

"Yes. His name is Wallace, and he knows it. I named him after our cowboy, who is long and lean, and the pig was long and lean when he came here. But he isn't lean any more."

"Oh, that's a good name. I thought of naming him Polka Dot, but then I'd be calling him either Pokey or Dottie, and it wouldn't be right. Then I thought of Curly because of his tail."

"If his tail's curled, that means he is happy. I'm so glad you phoned. Do you have a horse to ride? Wallace loves to follow along if it's a nice cool day. Perhaps you could bring him to visit me."

"Oh, I'd love to. I'll try to do that just as soon as Wallace knows for sure that he is my pig and won't try to run away."

Molly was happy. She turned away from the phone to tell Bert about the nice child who had won her pig.

"I told you he'd get a good home," Bert said.

"But he might not have. He's just a lucky pig, thank goodness."

Just as Christina had hoped, Alberto was willing to help build a pen for Wallace. "This is one smart pig," he told her. "Mostly you can't lead a pig with the rope around his neck. They tie him up by the leg."

Days were growing longer as summer approached, and there was plenty of light left after Alberto had finished his chores. Every ranch has a stockpile of used lumber and fence posts, and from this Christina helped Alberto choose boards and posts. They had decided to build Wallace's house and pen in the pony's pasture, where an oak tree could be at one corner of the pen. The tree could serve two purposes, as a strong corner post and as a summer shade. Furthermore, it was near the pony's watering trough, so that Christina had not far to carry water buckets to keep inside the pen for Wallace. In the fall the tree would drop acorns, which Wallace would enjoy eating.

At first sight the pony didn't like Wallace. He was not accustomed to knowing a pig, and he was half frightened. He put back his ears, blew a startled blast at the pig, and stood ready to run if he came near.

On a spring evening, when the low sun spread deep gold on green grass, Alberto and Christina started digging fence-post holes. Christina had the fence-post-hole digger, but Alberto could always sink a post hole quicker with just a shovel and a bar, in the old-fashioned way. The earth was still soft from the last rain, so that digging was easy. Alberto could dig three post holes to Christina's one.

Wallace was with them, enjoying the smell of the newly dug earth, rooting about in grass and leaves under his tree. He was pleased to be outside the box stall, where he had to live nights and while Christina was in school. She didn't turn him loose unless she could be with him. All day he could scarcely wait to see her, and when she opened the door and let him trot to her, he made little whispering sounds that expressed his fondness for her. "Ca-ca-ca," he said softly, lifting his round snout up toward her face.

Christina was learning that a pig has a great number of things to say and a great many ways of expressing his feelings. Wallace could grunt and croon with pleasure, squeal with annoyance until his voice grew ever higher, mutter contentedly to himself as he went about rooting in the earth, make surprised questioning little sounds and really startled blasting whistles if he were alarmed. He scolded loudly and got an anxious, quavering note in his voice if she were slow to feed him, and the times when he got mad and shrieked were when she shut him firmly in the box stall and went away. He tore at the door, but it wouldn't open.

The best way to leave him, she found, was to give him something delicious to eat and then hurry away while he was still enjoying it. For this purpose she saved all the table scraps and vegetable peelings and bread crusts. Wallace liked apple cores, too—and sugar lumps.

When the post holes were dug, Alberto dropped each heavy post into its place and held it upright while Christina shoveled in the dirt and tamped it with the bar. "You got to firm the earth good," he insisted. "Go slow, take plenty of time, push it down all hard around the post. Most people, they get in too big the hurry. The secret of the good fence is you got to tamp good around the posts. Else they don't stand good and solid, and after a while you see them leaning a little. You just shovel in only a little bit of dirt at a time, then you poke it down good and hard, and then put in a little more dirt."

Christina shoveled and tamped and shoveled and tamped, thumping away with the heavy bar until her arms and shoulders ached. But for Wallace, it was worth it.

"When I was a little boy, I had a little pig," Alberto told her. "Such a smart little pig. He went everywhere I went. So I taught him some tricks."

"Tricks!" said Christina, stopping work in amazement. "What kind of tricks?"

"Oh, he would sit down when I said to, and he would shake hands. He would lay down, and he would roll over. I made him a rope harness, and he pulled a little cart. So when I gathered wood, my pig, he haul it home."

"How wonderful!" Christina was entranced.

"Let me tell you, the pig he is one smart animal."

"Oh, I know. What happened to your little pig?"

"We ate him," said Alberto laconically.

Chapter Eight

Wallace's pen, when it was finished, was large enough so that he had plenty of room to wander around, and he had both sun and shade. There was a three-sided house that he could go in and out of as he chose. It had no floor, but Christina put down straw bedding into which he could cuddle at night. Alberto tossed in some empty feed sacks, because a pig likes to cover up his face with something like that on a cold night. Needless to say, Wallace kept his house clean. No pig wants his bed to be the least bit soiled.

At first he liked his pen very much. It was better than being shut up in the box stall, where there was no good rooting. After he had rooted up all the pasture grass in his pen, he began to wish to be outside it. He tried shoving at the boards that fenced him in, but Alberto had known how to construct a strong pig fence. Wallace squealed discontentedly, and the pony came and looked at him. Button was growing accustomed to having a pig living inside his pasture.

Wallace was lonely, so he said, "Ca-ca-ca," to the pony. The pony didn't seem to mind. He was lonely, too, and would like to have been out in the big pasture with the horses. Christina wouldn't turn him out because she was afraid that some of the larger animals would pick on him or that if he did make friends with one, that might happen to be the next one to be sold. It was better, anyway, to keep him in the small pasture where she wouldn't have to hunt for him when she wanted to ride him or pet him or brush him.

Button was smart and inquisitive, as ponies usually are. Gradually he and the pig came to be on very good terms with each other. Just as people want to touch things with their hands, so the pony wanted to feel with his nose. He leaned over the fence to snuffle along Wallace's back. Then he nibbled, very gently, and this felt good to Wallace. He grunted with pleasure.

Every afternoon after school, Christina hurried to change into jeans, and then she headed for the pony's pasture. She let Wallace out to wander around until suppertime, and she brushed both Wallace and Button.

One afternoon she saddled Button and called Wallace. She wanted to find out how well he would follow, because some day soon she wanted to take him to call on Mrs. Ames.

There was no problem. As she rode out one of the ranch roadways, Wallace came scampering along. She put the pony to a lope and looked back to see the pig galloping, his tail curling and uncurling with the motion of his haunches, his ears flapping gaily.

She stopped the pony to let him have a few bites of extra-lush grass, and Wallace, snout close to pony nose, helped himself to the good forage, too.

When Christina rode on, Wallace lingered for a few extra bites, then trotted to catch up, squealing querulously because he really wanted to eat some more.

It turned out to be such a delightful short trip that Christina resolved to take Wallace visiting soon. When Saturday came, she asked Alberto what he was going to do that day.

"We got this colt that needs riding. I been training him in the ring. Now I got to take him out on the trail."

"Oh, goody! I want to go riding on Button and take Wallace along. Do you suppose we could ride over to Ameses'?"

"Why not? There's a trail across the hills. Take us maybe one half hour, maybe forty-five minutes. It's cool enough —won't hurt the pig none."

Christina hurried to get Button and Wallace while Alberto caught and saddled the colt. She was ready before he was. The colt eyed the pig with alarm, and Alberto laughed at him. "Behave now. That pig ain't gonna hurt you."

Alberto was the best horse trainer in the county. Christina admired the way he handled any horse. Casually he seemed to assume that an animal was going to do just what he wanted it to, and the horse always realized this. The colt sashayed around a bit uneasily when he mounted, snorting at Wallace, and Alberto said, "Come on now, behave yourself." The colt did.

The colt was a beautiful red quarter horse, three years old, and it was an adventure for him to be ridden outside the training ring and, of all things, to be accompanied by a pig.

"Good for a colt to see all sorts of things different," Alberto remarked.

It was a beautiful ride. Late April is the very best time in California, with grass and wild flowers shining bright. From time to time, Wallace had to stop to eat something extra good, and when, puffing and anxious to catch up, he came at a gallop, the quarter horse jumped nervously. "You'll get used to this and everything else pretty soon," Alberto told him.

They rode through a canyon between hills, came to open meadows where the hills drew back, and rode over a rise and down a little slope. Wallace took some good sniffs of familiar air and hurried on ahead. "Why, he knows where he's going," Christina exclaimed delightedly.

He did. He saw the barn and the house. The dog, Lucy, saw riders approach and barked and hurried toward them as they stopped to open a gate. Wallace said, "Ca-ca-ca," and trotted to Lucy, who waved her long tail and licked his face. Dog and pig went on toward the house.

Molly Ames came out on the back porch. "Why, Wallace!" she exclaimed, and bent down. Wallace promptly flopped to have his belly rubbed. Besides, he was tired, and it felt good to lie down.

"Oh, I'm so glad to see this pig again," Molly said as Alberto and Christina rode up. "I was really sure he wasn't going to have a good home. You must be Christina, and I know Alberto. He's helped my husband with the cattle sometimes."

Alberto tipped his hat politely and dismounted. "You can tie to that tree," Molly said. "Can I get you some milk or soda pop or something else to drink?"

"We better stay where I can watch this colt. He might pull back, though he shouldn't. Here, Christina, you tie your pony beside him to keep him quiet," and Alberto took down his tie rope from the saddle.

"I never knew a pig before," Christina told Molly. "I really didn't know what fun a pig can be. I felt so sorry for Wallace when the kids were chasing him that I had to catch him to save him."

"Oh, I'm so glad! He might have gone to a dreadful home."

They sat on the back-porch steps in the sun, and Molly brought out cool drinks. Wallace rooted a little bed for himself and lay down to rest. He was a happy pig. Lucy cuddled beside him.

"Why couldn't you keep him?" Christina wanted to know.

"Well, I'll tell you, Christina. When you're a little girl, you think that when you are grown, you can be your own boss. But you aren't. You grow up and get married, and there are times when it's much easier to do what your husband suggests. I really wanted to keep Wallace, but it was very difficult. Anyhow, it all turned out all right. I'm just delighted that Wallace is yours."

"Oh, so am I. I hope I can keep him forever."

"I hope so, too. I had a little pig. She was a runt that didn't get enough milk from her mother. All her brothers and sisters were too big and strong and pushed her away. She'd have starved. She was so tiny at first that she could stand with all four feet on one of my hands. I raised her on a bottle, and she was the cutest little thing. I had to keep her in the house where it was warm, and we had a towel for her to lie on. She loved that towel and dragged it wherever she went, and then she'd root it into a bed when she wanted to go to sleep.

"And one day, for the first time, I put down a pan of water for her. She got all excited and squealed and poked the pan with her nose and some water splashed out on her, and she shrieked with joy and went into a bouncy little dance around and around it. After that she always wanted to play in water."

"Oh, I wish I'd had Wallace when he was that tiny! What happened to your little pig?" Christina asked.

"Oh, she grew big and had piglets of her own. Litter after litter of the best little pigs. We lived on a farm in the Middle West and raised all kinds of animals."

"Alberto had a pig, too. He did tricks. But they ate him."

45

"I had many sisters and brothers, and down in Mexico we were very poor and hungry," Alberto explained.

"Yes," said Molly, "that can happen. Oh, I see Bert and Wallace riding into the corral. I want them to see the pig."

The men unsaddled and turned out their horses and came walking to the back porch. "Well, look what's here," Bert said while Wallace stood grinning at his namesake.

Wallace the pig opened one eye and made his usual remark. "Erful," he said, and went contentedly back to sleep.

Christina giggled. "He always says that everything is 'erful.' "

Wallace the cowboy stepped into the kitchen and brought out a pan of water. The pig wakened and drank thirstily. "See, you forgot to give the little fellow a drink," Wallace scolded.

Molly said, "You must all stay for lunch."

Alberto stood up. "Thank you very much. But no. We have to go back. I have another colt to ride this afternoon, and Christina's mama, she expects her."

"Next time you must all stay for lunch, then," Molly insisted. "Come back soon."

"Oh, we will." Christina mounted her pony. "Come on, Wallace. We have to go home now."

Wallace grunted sleepily. Bert shoved him with his foot. Wallace stood up, hurried up the porch steps, and settled down on the blanket he used to share with Lucy.

"Oh, Wallace!" Christina wailed. "You don't want to come home with me!"

"Of course he does. He's just tired and sleepy," Molly explained, "and this is all familiar to him."

Bert shooed the pig off the porch, and Wallace the cowboy swatted him with his hat. Wallace went fast in a circle and ended up on the porch.

"A pig is the hardest thing to herd," Molly said. "One pig you just can't chase anywhere. They turn and dart so fast."

"Here," said Alberto, "you put your lead rope on the pig, Christina, and you hand me your pony. I'll lead the pony, and you walk and lead the pig until we get on a little ways. Then he'll come along with us when you turn him loose."

At first Wallace didn't want to lead, but a few shoves from Bert's boot got him started. "I see why they call some people pigheaded," Bert remarked.

Molly laughed. "A pig can be a most determined creature. But bring him to visit again, Christina."

"Yes," Christina promised, feeling happy that both she and Wallace had Molly for a friend, though it still seemed odd to her that Molly had let herself be talked out of keeping her pig. Adults are very difficult to understand. Anyway, it was obvious that Molly was pleased with Wallace's present situation in life and obvious that she had been worried about him.

On the other side of the gate, Christina untied the pig. He came along willingly, so she got back on Button.

"Alberto," she asked, "do you suppose that Wallace could learn tricks?"

"But of course. He is one smart pig."

"How do you teach a pig?"

"Like a dog. You got to be patient. Keep after him, and then pet him or give him something to eat when he does right. It takes a little time."

"Would you help me?"

"Sure."

Chapter Nine

CHRISTINA had a dream.

Wallace was going to become a great and famous pig. She decided that people should be taught about pigs. It would be Wallace's mission in life to prove to the world that a pig is a clever and charming animal.

The idea had begun to grow when Alberto had told her of his pig that learned to do tricks.

Wallace could be educated to the point where she could show him in a trained pig act, and at the next fair he would be the star performer. Instead of being a frightened greased pig to be chased around, Wallace, with aplomb and confidence, would put on an act to amaze everyone.

Already Christina could hear the applause and the cheers and the cries of wonderment from astonished spectators. By his brilliance Wallace might be able to help less fortunate pigs; perhaps after seeing him, a few people would be inspired to give their pigs better living conditions.

Christina felt like a crusader in a great cause. She daydreamed about her trained pig at school and went to sleep thinking about him at night.

"Alberto," she said on an afternoon when her friend had found time to help with Wallace's first lesson. "let's keep this a secret for a while. Let's not tell a soul until Wallace is all trained. Then we will surprise everyone."

"Yes, that is good. Now, the first thing to teach a pig is the easiest thing. Make him go down. Any pig that's kind of tame will almost do this by himself, to get the belly rubbed. You say to him, 'Down,' and push a little, and when he is down, rub him and give him a bite."

"Wallace, lie down, down, Wallace." Christina reached a hand to Wallace's pink belly, and down he went. She rewarded him with praise and petting and a bit of sugar. After he was up, she tried it again, and he obeyed at once. Soon she had only to tap the earth with her hand, say, "Down, Wallace," and he bent his knees and sank.

Christina was delighted. "Now shall we teach him to sit and shake hands or to roll over?"

"No," said Alberto. "This is enough for one day. See how well he knows this tomorrow. It is like training the colt, only a little at one time so's they won't get tired of doing it. Go and take him for a little walk now."

They wandered around the bright green pasture, and the pony followed along, for he liked company. Wallace rooted the grass, ate a few flowers, and then, feeling refreshed with the coolness of late afternoon, exclaimed "Whoosh!" and scampered in a circle around his friends. This excited Button, who began to remember what fun it had been to be a colt, and he made a few playful leaps over the grass.

"Come on, run!" cried Christina, feeling like a colt herself, and with Wallace blasting away excitedly, the three of them ran to the far fence, where both animals stopped to huff and puff and Christina sprawled on the grass. Wallace lay down beside her, the pony put down his head to snuffle at her hair, and Christina felt one of those glad, happy moments that comes with a feeling of nearness to earth and animals.

Wallace had a warm animal grassy smell. Button had the sharp salty-sweet fragrance of horses, and his breath smelled of grass and grain.

Lazily Christina sat up and began counting the dark dots on Wallace. There were exactly fifty-one of them. "I must remember that," she thought. "It's good identification in case he ever gets lost." Not that she expected Wallace to ever be lost. He liked his home too much to stray from it.

The next afternoon Wallace had another lesson. He ended up by being forced to learn the first lesson all over again.

What happened was that Christina asked him to lie down twice, and he obeyed. The third time he didn't want to, and when Christina patted the earth and said, "Down," he merely pressed his snout firmly against the earth and stood.

"Oh, come on, Wallace, down," she persisted, and finally he bent his knees and stayed in that position.

"Well, that's a good trick, Alberto. We can tell him to say his prayers when he does this."

"Yes, that is a good trick for later. But now he must learn to do what you tell him. He will have to go down and stay down until you tell him to get up."

Wallace rose from his knees and again pressed snout to earth when Christina demanded that he get down. He looked stubborn and determined beyond anything, hoofs and snout appearing to be glued to the ground. Christina tried pushing him on down, but she couldn't.

Her persistence annoyed him. He had a temper tantrum, squalling like a bad child and stamping his feet.

"Stop that now," Alberto commanded, and forcefully put the screaming pig down.

"Oh, dear," said Christina, losing hope in Wallace's ability to be trained.

"He'll be all right," said Alberto. "He's got to learn to mind."

The complaining sounds gradually ceased and changed to a contented rhythmic grunting as Wallace enjoyed having his belly rubbed.

When he tried to get up, Alberto wouldn't let him.

"You wait until we say so," Alberto told him.

Finally Wallace was allowed up, only to be made to go down again and to stay there until he had permission to stand up.

When he discovered that he was forced to go down, whether he was in the mood or not, and that, once down, he was rewarded, Wallace stopped protesting. After all, this wasn't an unpleasant thing to be doing, and certainly he was getting lots of attention.

The next afternoon Christina had no trouble. She said, "Down," and Wallace sprawled in the grass.

"Next we will teach him to sit down like a dog sits," Alberto announced.

Since a pig is an animal that often sits of its own accord, this proved only a little more difficult than making him lie down. After Alberto had pushed and bent him into position several times, with both of them demanding, "Sit," he knew what he was to do. He looked charming, posed on his curved haunches, his front legs straightly braced, points of ears in front of his eyes. Christina sat down beside him and gave him a hug.

Wallace had decided that his education was more fun than not, since he was fond of praise and attention and sugar lumps. He became such a satisfactory pupil that Alberto grew more enthusiastic than ever and took time off at noon to work with him a little.

Chapter Ten

JUST before it was time for the grass to turn brown, heavy rains came to California, and Wallace stayed sleeping in his house, snout and eyes buried under the empty feed sacks. He liked covering himself up when the weather was cold and damp. The rain on his roof made a pleasant sound that mingled with his dreams, and he was the coziest pig in the land.

His education was neglected for a few days, but when again the sun shown on the sparkling grass, he remembered what he had learned. He could sit and shake hands, he could bend his knees and say his prayers, he could lie down and roll over, and he could play dead. Before the Fourth of July, he was going to have to learn other tricks, because Christina was hopeful that he could perform at the little Fourth of July celebration in town. If he could do six or seven tricks, that would be enough for his debut. Later they would think of other, more ambitious things to teach him. Alberto thought that perhaps they could work the pony into the act some way.

Wallace had reached the point where he seemed really to want to learn. Perhaps it was that he realized that he had to do what he was told. At any rate, he appeared eager to please and tried to do what was asked of him. His trainers had gotten it through his pig mind that once they started to show him how to do a trick, they would not stop until he had mastered it. A pig is naturally inclined to be lazy, and Wallace discovered that it was less work to do what was demanded than to put up an argument.

The rains that were so good for pastures had also made little streams run. A shiny brook wandered in and out of the pony's pasture, and Christina and Wallace went wading in it. The pig rooted at the sandy bottom, his face buried to his eyes, remarkable burbling sounds coming from his immersed snout. He stayed clean and sparkling from all the splashing about.

By the day in June when summer vacation began, the pasture grass had dried to bright gold, and the hills were tawny. Only one pool was left in the pony's pasture, and it would not last out the summer.

Now that Christina didn't have to go to school, her pig received more schooling than ever. The lovely long days were perfect for this. Every evening after supper, Christina took Wallace to Alberto's bunkhouse, and there by the back door the pig's education proceeded.

Christina had a big beach ball, and the texture of it was just right to please a pig's snout. Wallace enjoyed rolling it about, and after he had played with it a little, it was not difficult to teach him to roll it to Christina. He learned that as soon as he had pushed the ball to her, he would receive a sugar lump, so when she threw the ball, he scampered after it and rolled it back to her.

Though a pig is not much of a jumping animal, he is a bouncing animal, and Alberto decided that Wallace could learn to jump through a hoop. First he was allowed to step through to receive his sugar. Then the hoop was raised each time until he had to hop. If he tried to run around it or squeeze under, he did not receive his reward, and when he became aware of this, he jumped quite well.

Christina thought of the next trick. Since Wallace could push a ball, he could push a doll buggy. It was all the same principle. She found her old doll buggy and a discarded doll, and that trick became a success, too. Wallace had only to push the buggy handle with his snout and keep it rolling a little, and then he received his sugar lump.

Now he knew seven tricks that he must practice twice each day to keep his performance perfect.

"This will be enough for the Fourth of July," Alberto decided. "Later we can show him more things. Maybe we can get a little cart for him to pull. We should have taught him to make a bow—go down on one knee at the end of the show when the people clap, but I forgot that, and it's too late to start now. He'll do that for the next time."

"Oh, I hope that the Fourth of July won't be too hot. It mostly is. On a very hot day, it would be hard on Wallace. I guess," said Christina, "now that time's growing short, we must show my mother and father what Wallace can do. They'll have to help me get him to town and back in the pickup. I know that they'll want to as soon as they see how wonderful Wallace is."

"Tomorrow night after supper would be a good time," Alberto suggested. "Tell them you got a surprise for them if they come out on the front lawn after they eat."

At table the next evening, Christina announced, "There will be a wonderful show after dinner, out on the lawn. It's going to be a big surprise for you."

At first it was—for Christina and Alberto, anyway. Wallace would do nothing but root enthusiastically at the juicy lawn grass.

"I'm stupido!" Alberto moaned, clapping his hand to his head. "No. Not here. We go to the corral where the ground is bare."

On the way to the corral, once they got on hard earth, Wallace pushed the doll buggy. Christina's mother thought that a wonderful show and that that was the whole surprise.

"Just you wait," Christina exulted. "He can do lots more."

"Well, what do you know!" said her father, growing more interested.

The audience of two perched on the corral fence while Christina and her assistant put Wallace through his paces. "Darling, this is simply wonderful!" her mother kept exclaiming. "I had no idea that a pig could learn so much."

"When we take horses to the big County Fair in the fall, you and the pig could do an act. The fair might even pay you for the entertainment."

Christina stared at her father in amazement. This was an angle that hadn't occurred to her. "Pay me? How much?"

"Fifty dollars perhaps, or a hundred. Probably you can make the act even better by then."

"Oh, we can. Alberto has lots more ideas." Christina glowed. She was not only proving her point that a pig is clever, but she was also making the ownership of Wallace a practical and worthwhile venture from the adult point of view. This had not entered into her dreams before. She said, "What we planned to do first is to show him at the Fourth of July celebration."

Her mother said, "We must polish up the doll buggy and decorate the wheels with ribbons. The hoop, too. And bathe

the pig, and couldn't we put gilt on his hoofs? But what about you, Christina? You're so easily embarrassed. You won't even take part in a school play."

"This is different, though. No one will even look at me. They'll all be looking at Wallace. I won't even be thinking about *me*."

With her parents so enthusiastic, the whole project was growing better and better. Christina thought of something else. "We must tell Mrs. Ames to be sure and come to the show."

Chapter Eleven

This time Wallace was not put into a crate for his trip to town. He was too big for that. The ranch pickup was backed against a bank, and Christina led him onto the truck bed and rode with him. Though this Fourth of July was not scorching hot, it was warm, and as they rode along, the breeze felt refreshing.

Christina's father had made arrangements for the performance, which was to be at three in the afternoon in the very ring where Wallace, as a greased pig, had been chased.

Her mother, now deep in the spirit of the thing, had helped with Wallace's bathing and decoration. She had insisted on gilding his hoofs. He looked beautiful. Around his neck he was to wear a red, white, and blue ribbon, which was to be adjusted and tied into a bow just before his appearance.

The doll buggy and the hoop were decorated with the red, white, and blue ribbon, in honor of the holiday.

As for Christina, her mother had decided that she should look like a farm boy, so she wore bib overalls, a checked blue-and-white shirt, and a straw hat.

"Blue goes good on you, with your brown eyes and hair. Blue and brown are good together," Mrs. Wood observed.

"But no one will look at me with Wallace there," Christina insisted happily. It was good that she felt this way. Otherwise, she would have been weak with shyness.

For the occasion Alberto wore his purple silk shirt with the fancy buttons, new jeans, and his well-polished high-heeled boots.

They arrived, as they had planned, at the grounds on the edge of town shortly before time for the act to begin so that they wouldn't have to wait around in the crowd.

Christina shook with excitement, and Alberto laughed at her. "Don't be so nervous. This pig, he'll know what to do."

"But I'm scared."

"Well I'm not, and I don't think the pig is. Come on. I'll take the stuff to the ring. You bring the pig."

"I think he is scared," Christina said.

Wallace's ribbon was now tied around his neck into a big crisp bow. He had worn it for a while every day to get accustomed to it. He also wore a lead rope, which would be removed in the ring. As Christina led him the short way from the truck to the ring, Wallace crowded close to her legs.

Just before their entrance, Christina heard the announcer telling about this trained pig and his owner, and almost before she realized it, she and Wallace and Alberto were in the ring. She took off the rope and stood back to give Wallace his first command.

The people laughed and applauded.

Wallace froze.

There was something familiar about this and not good. He did not remember the exact details of what had happened before, but he remembered his terror. It began to engulf him again.

There was only one thing to do, and he did it. He ran for his life.

"Wallace!" Christina cried desperately, but he was gone.

The crowd parted before him, each individual fearful of being knocked down by the speeding animal. At the edge of the crowd, two little boys gave chase, and that only accelerated the speed of Wallace's departure.

People were laughing about the trained pig that knew only how to run away, but Christina didn't hear them. She started running toward the place where Wallace had disappeared. Anything bad could happen now. In his fright Wallace could run blindly in front of a car. Or someone might think it funny to steal the pig and make off with him. She might never see him again. These thoughts tore through her mind, and she hoped for some sight of him, hoped that someone had had the presence of mind to grab him and hold him for her.

Her father and Alberto jumped in the pickup and went driving up and down the streets of town, cutting across vacant lots, sure that they would catch sight of the pig somewhere. He couldn't simply vanish.

But he had.

Christina stopped running because she couldn't run one more step. She was gasping, and her heart was pounding.

"Have you seen a pig?" she kept asking everyone she met.

She saw her father and Alberto, and they, seeing her, yelled and stopped. "Get in," her father said. "No use walking. We'll drive around and find him pretty soon."

"Probably he got tired and found a place to hide. He'll come out after a while," Alberto assured her.

"He was headed toward town, not away. And that's bad."

"Well, you can't lose a pig that easily," her father said comfortingly. "What scared him anyway?"

"The people, I guess. He must have remembered that other time. I'd never thought about that. Oh, we should have rehearsed him in front of more people," Christina wailed. "It's all my fault."

"Maybe we better go back and have them announce over the loudspeaker for people to keep an eye open for him."

"And offer a reward for anyone who finds him," Christina added.

Chapter Twelve

RECKLESS in his flight, Wallace scurried across the town's Main Street. Main Street was a state highway, and traffic was heavy because of the holiday. By luck Wallace crossed at an intersection. A pig with golden hoofs, wearing a red, white, and blue ribbon, was not a common sight, and traffic came to a startled halt.

His direction took him up a side street. Then he darted down an alley, saw a trash can in the shade of a pepper tree, and gratefully crept behind the can to hide and rest. He hadn't been noticed entering the alley because nearly everyone was at the Fourth of July celebration. He was hot, thirsty, and tired. He breathed heavily, and his heart pounded.

If his rest had not been interrupted, he would have stayed there until it was nearly dark. Then he would have tried to find his way home.

But down the alley came two characters carrying cans of beer in their arms and much beer within them. They were celebrating the Fourth of July. If they hadn't been celebrating the Fourth of July, they would have been celebrating something else. They lived in a shack along the alleyway, and they were always celebrating something. Whenever they got a few days' work, honest or otherwise, they had money enough to buy something to drink, and then they had a fine time. They thought it funny to pretend to be Mexicans, which they were not. They called themselves Pancho and Pedro, and they spoke to each other in the way that they thought Mexicans talked.

"Pancho," said the fat one, who called himself Pedro, "what is this I hear? Something seems to be breathing."

"It is a pig," said Pancho, stopping short and peering around the trash can. "Here, you hold the beer, quick. This is one fine, fat pig. We will eat him."

Wallace had not jumped up and run because these people had approached slowly, and he was not really afraid of human beings ordinarily. But soon he wished that he had left.

Before he realized it, the one called Pancho had hold of his back legs, and he found himself reluctantly walking on his front hoofs, being pushed along and steered by the holder of his back legs. His screams pierced the air, but they went unheard by anyone who might have been able to rescue him.

"See, this is how you move the pig. You push him like the wheelbarrow."

"Pancho, where do we take him?"

"We take him into the house to hide him. Then we will kill him."

"Not in our house. Not in our fine house."

"Where else do you say? We have no pen for the pig. And if we did, someone might see him there. Someone might steal our pig. No, Pedro. The pig he goes into the house."

And he did. Unfortunately the shack was very near.

Once inside, Wallace was released, and his screams ceased immediately. This was better, and he wandered about nosing the empty cans and bottles that littered the floor.

"Poor little one, he is thirsty," said Pancho, and tipped his

beer can above Wallace's nose. Wallace lifted his snout and drank.

"Pancho!" cried Pedro, horrified. "Do not give our good beer to the pig."

"Can't you see he is thirsty? And this may well be his last Fourth of July on this earth. Here, open for him another can."

"He is a handsome little pig," Pedro admitted, "and what a nice ribbon he wears. And look at his gold feet."

"He will be handsome cooked with the apple in his mouth."

"No, Pancho, this pig is too big for that. We will make of him the chops and roasts. He will be so good."

"Poor little one," said Pancho. "It is too hot to kill a pig today."

Pedro agreed. "I know what we will do. Tomorrow morning, very early, before the sun when it is cool, that would be a better pig-killing time."

"When everyone is asleep. Yes, we can take him out in the yard. It will be good and cool."

"Listen!" exclaimed Pedro, and peered nervously toward the window. "See, here comes a truck. A pickup. Perhaps someone is looking for our pig."

"Give the pig some more beer, quick, so he will say nothing."

While Wallace consumed a can of beer, Christina and her father and Alberto proceeded slowly down the alley, looking on this side and that. Several cars had driven through the alley since Wallace had been in the shack, and his tracks had been smeared over.

"I think we should give up for now," her father told Christina. "It's growing late, and it'll get dark."

"No, Daddy! Keep looking."

"He's hiding," said Alberto. "We'll find him tomorrow."

"Oh, please! We've got to find him tonight!"

"Your poor mother," said Mr. Wood. "Still waiting for us at the grounds."

"I bet she isn't. I bet she and some friends are looking for Wallace."

At last darkness ended the search. They drove back to the fair grounds and found Christina's mother—she and Molly Ames had been looking for Wallace—and they went home sadly.

Christina, unable to eat, went to bed, and then, of course, she couldn't sleep.

Chapter Thirteen

Wallace was enjoying himself. His captors grew more mellow and more generous with every can of beer that they drank, and Wallace seemed to get at least half of every can.

Wallace began to find it difficult to walk about. Finally he leaned against the wall and sang something to himself. Then he sank down and went to sleep.

His companions went to sleep, too. For a time there was no sound in the shack but that of robust snoring.

Later a big moon rose. It was a waning moon, but still large and bright. Its light came through the open window and glowed on the silvery polka-dot pig. It wakened him.

He wanted a drink of water, and his head hurt.

He stood up and wandered about. He went to the door. It was only a fragile screen door fastened with a hook. Wallace pushed.

The hook gave way. The door pushed open, and Wallace stepped out into the warm, bright night. He didn't linger to savor the sweet-smelling air. Talking softly to himself, he wandered up the alley.

Something came to his attention. His nostrils led him into a back-yard garden where a big, overripe watermelon had cracked open. Grunting with satisfaction, Wallace ate every bit of it. Next he found a corn patch and ate all of that, and after he had rooted up a strawberry bed, he was ready to head for the hills and home.

He was not exactly sure where home was, but anyway he wanted to get back to where things smelled more familiar. Even in town he could smell the direction of sage-covered hills.

No people were stirring about. Some dogs barked at him, but he ignored them, and they did not give chase. There was not one car on Main Street where he crossed it, and he chose Third Street, which headed south. There he found a lawn to enjoy before he went on. The pavement ended, and he followed a dirt road, and that ended. Beyond were the hills, and Wallace trudged into the brush, where he lost his bright ribbon.

After a while he grew tired and rooted himself a bed under a sumac and went to sleep.

Early the next day, Christina and her father and Alberto headed for town, where again they drove up streets and alleys and across vacant lots. When they proceeded along the alley where Pedro and Pancho lived, Alberto cried, "Hey, stop! Looks like tracks here."

No cars had yet been through the unpaved alley, and in the dust were Wallace's tracks. Everyone jumped out of the truck and followed the tracks to where they turned into a back yard.

Wallace was not there, but the irate owner was. Despairingly, he was examining his ruined vegetable patch.

"Have you seen a pig?" Christina asked nervously.

The man glowered. "Some pig has been in here all right. Did about twenty dollars' worth of damage to my garden. Would that be your pig?"

"How do we know?" asked Alberto craftily. "We saw no pig in your garden and neither did you."

"If we find that it was our pig, of course we'll pay the damages," Christina said. "We are looking for a spotted pig. Let us know if you see him. We've got to find him."

"If I see him first, I'll shoot the danged thing!"

"Oh, please don't!" This was a danger that Christina hadn't thought about. It was possible that some angry gardener would shoot a marauding animal. "Oh, please!" she implored.

"It would please me very much," said the man, "to make a sieve out of that pig."

Christina's father was growing angry. "You aren't being very reasonable," he said. "This happens to be a valuable animal that escaped by accident." He turned away. "Come on," he said to Christina and Alberto. "Let's get out of here."

They went back toward the truck and met the ones who called themselves Pedro and Pancho wandering along the alley.

"Have you seen a pig?" Christina asked eagerly.

"What kind of pig?"

"Silver with dark dots. We are offering a reward to anyone who finds him."

The two looked at each other. Pancho shook his head sadly. "No, we didn't see any pig. But how big is the reward? Maybe we could help."

"Twenty dollars?" suggested Christina timidly. She didn't own twenty dollars, but surely Alberto and her father would advance her the money.

"Twenty dollars!" exclaimed Pedro, thinking of the money in terms of liquid refreshment. "Yes, we will look for that pig. But where do we look, Pancho?"

"Oh, around." And the two sauntered on.

68

"I don't think they'll find him," said Christina's father. "They don't look very ambitious."

"At least they're better than that man with the garden."

Alberto had been tracking. "After he got out of the garden, he walked along the alley that way. Maybe we'll see him in another garden further on."

But they didn't. The tracks proceeded to a paved street, and they found no further trace of Wallace that day.

Chapter Fourteen

I N the middle of the morning, Wallace woke up and stirred from the shade of his sumac bush. It was hot in the sunshine, and again he was thirsty. For a while he rooted around and ate some weeds and dry grass, but what he wanted was a good drink of water.

Trails went everywhere through the brush, and Wallace's golden hoofs found a worn one that went along a side hill and dipped into a little draw. He began to hurry, for now he was sure that he smelled water, and he made eager comments as he trotted along.

He came to a small clearing in a shallow canyon and hurried past bites of green grass toward a willow tree and a boulder. From under the boulder, water seeped and formed into a pool. Gratefully Wallace dunked his snout. When finally he had enough to drink, he wallowed in the pool, cooling first one side of himself and then the other.

This was nearly as good as home, except that he began to feel lonesome. Here was no pony, no Christina, no Alberto.

Wallace had no mental picture of what he himself looked like, but he did know what his own pen looked like. He knew the surrounding trees and rocks and lay of the land. In a way he identified himself with familiar surroundings, so that the things he knew were part of himself, and without familiar sights he felt strange.

After several days, Wallace had made no progress in the direction of home. Without intending it to be so, the area of the spring became his base camp, for every time he headed for someplace else, thirst drove him back to the pool by the willow. He was as confined as though he were inside a good fence.

Christina had made no progress in the direction of Wallace, either. She worried and moaned, kept pestering her parents and Alberto to do something further, and had dreary telephone conversations with Molly Ames, who was doing what searching she could.

"I don't know what more we can do," Mr. Wood said. "We've looked everywhere we can and put an ad in the paper. I bet he'll come home one of these days."

Secretly Christina's father thought that Wallace was forever gone. No doubt someone had eaten the pig by now, but he didn't want to say that to Christina. He felt very sorry for his grieving child. So did Christina's mother. Both parents did their best to comfort her and kept telling her that surely Wallace would show up somewhere sometime soon.

It was Alberto who made the most helpful suggestion, partly because he thought that Christina should do something other than mope around and worry.

"Why don't you get on your pony," he suggested, "and cut through the hills in the direction of town? That is one smart pig, and he's probably trying to come home across the hills. You might pick up his tracks somewhere, even if you don't see him right at first."

"But what about fences?" asked Christina. "The only time I rode that direction, I kept getting into cow pastures."

"Wherever there's fences, there's gates somewhere. Just keep following the fence line and you'll come to some kind

72

of gate, or come to somewheres where you can unwind some wires easy. But be sure and put them back up. People get mad if you leave any fences down."

"I'll do that!" Christina agreed, glad to have something to do. "I'll go ask Mama right now."

Alberto added, "There's a little canyon cuts down through the hills in that direction. Maybe it's too brushy and rocky to follow all the way, but keep near it. It goes the way you'll be wanting to go."

It was too late in the day to start out then, but the next morning Christina got up early, made two jelly and peanut-butter sandwiches, took some oranges because they were easier to carry than water, and saddled Button.

"I know you won't get lost," said her mother, "because Button would always know the way home, but be careful about rattlesnakes. And don't dare stay away too long. I'll expect you home by the middle of the afternoon at least."

Hopefully Christina rode off.

Chapter Fifteen

THE pony was none too willing, but he was a good pony, accustomed to being obedient, so he jogged along where the going was good and trudged doggedly where the trail was rough and brushy.

As Alberto had predicted, Christina managed to find ways through from pasture to pasture. After she had traveled for nearly an hour, she started calling Wallace from time to time, for what if he were resting somewhere in the brush? If suddenly he should appear, she felt that she would tumble off Button from joy.

The canyon they had been following veered off to the left. It had become more rocky and brushy, so that it was easier to follow its general direction than to dip into it. Button traveled for about half an hour across a golden meadow before he approached a fence and a gate. The gate was locked.

Christina stared at the gate in dismay. Beyond was more or less open country, where brush was sparse and not very tall, and Christina looked with longing at a clear trail heading in the very direction she wanted to go. Then she looked at the fence wires and saw, on the corner post, that instead of being stapled, one set of wires had been firmly wound. It was all so tight that it looked hopeless, but anyway she slipped off Button to have a better look. Whoever had wound the wires had used pliers, and it wasn't going to be easy to get them undone. But perhaps with patience, strength, and determination she could do it.

Or perhaps she should look along the fence stretching to the south. Perhaps there would be one unlocked gate along there. This didn't seem likely. Why would anyone lock one gate and leave another unlocked?

She sighed and tried to get at least one place started.

Just then Button flung up his head and whinnied.

Christina looked, and there approaching on the other side of the fence were horses and riders. "Oh," she thought fearfully, "now someone's going to come along and bawl me out for trying to take a fence down."

But as the riders drew nearer, she saw that they were children. A pale-haired girl, about her own age, rode a little sorrel with a flaxen mane and tail. Another girl, who looked to be Indian, rode a silvery gray horse, and a brown-skinned boy rode a burro.

Button was looking with horror at the burro. Possibly he had seen burros before, but he didn't remember, and now he blew a loud, startled blast through his nostrils and tried to pull away from Christina and run home.

All the children laughed.

"Stop it, silly," Christina told Button. "I guess he's never seen a burro before," she said to the others.

"He's a cute little pony," the blond girl observed, and she spoke in such a friendly fashion that Christina, usually so shy, felt at ease.

"I'm looking for my pig. A silvery colored pig with dark polka dots. I don't suppose you've seen him anywhere?"

"Oh," said the friendly girl. "No. But is it that trick pig? I was there. I saw him get scared at the show and run away

75

from you. How awful! And you haven't found him yet?"

Christina shook her head sadly. "I don't even know where to look."

The girl on the silvery gray horse said, "I've seen you at school, I think. But we aren't in the same class."

"Yes, I remember. I guess I've seen all of you at school." She added, a little timidly, "My name's Christina Wood, and my father raises quarter horses."

The boy spoke up. "Yeah, I know where you live."

"I'm Kathy Evans," said the light-haired girl. "And this is Ginger. She lives on the Indian reservation. And Pete is her cousin. I live on a ranch over near the reservation."

Christina had never become acquainted with people under such easy circumstances. Usually she felt awkward and didn't know what to say when anyone was introduced.

Kathy said, "We'll help you look for your pig. We're just riding around for fun."

Christina looked hopelessly at the fence. "But how can I get through to ride with you?"

"That's easy," and Pete slid off the burro, took a small pair of pliers out of his pocket, and started unwinding wire.

"Pete can do almost anything," his cousin pointed out.

When Button and Christina were on the other side of the fence, Pete put the wires back up but didn't make them very tight. "I'll do them better after you get through on the way home."

Everything seemed much better to Christina now that she was not alone. "Say," said Pete after they'd ridden nearly a mile, "I know where there's lots of pigs. Some of them got spots. You know the other side of town, toward the road that goes to the coast, then you turn right up a dirt road and there's a bunch of hogs? I was there one day with my uncle.

76

He was going to buy a pig maybe. Anyway, what if your pig went there? He might of, on account of smelling other pigs. And maybe the people saw him outside the pens and thought he was one of theirs got loose, or maybe just took him. Anyway, he might be in there with all those."

"Oh, he might," said Christina. "Could we ride there from here?"

"We could, but it'd be a long ways."

"We'd have to cross a highway and go through the edge of town. I guess we shouldn't," Ginger pointed out.

"I know," said Christina. "I better go home and see if I can't get my mother or my father to drive me there in the car."

"Oh, I hope your pig's there," Kathy said sympathetically. "Let us know, anyway. If you don't find him, we'll all help look for him."

"We could ride with you lots of days," Ginger offered. "We'll find some short cut between your place and ours, or some place where we could all meet."

"It'll be our project," Kathy decreed. "For the summer. We'll play like detectives, and I bet we'll find your pig."

Christina waved good-by to her friends, and Button went loping across the meadow as Pete firmly wound the fence wires back into place.

It was unfortunate that the children couldn't know that if they had ridden further, they might have reached the area where Wallace was staying.

Chapter Sixteen

For the first time since she had lost her pig, Christina felt almost cheerful and hopeful. She was excited about finding such friendly children. For no particular reason she had never tried to find friends at school. Now, suddenly, life seemed to be expanding.

She reached home just as her parents were finishing a late lunch. "Mama, Daddy, can we go to town? I found out where there are a whole lot of pigs, and Wallace may be with them."

"I've got too much to do," her father said, "but maybe your mother will drive you in."

"Why yes, of course," her mother agreed. "Where did you find this out?"

"Oh, I met three of the nicest kids out riding. Pete, this one boy, told me where there's a pig farm on the other side of town, and Wallace may have wandered there. Can we go right away?"

"Did you eat your sandwiches?"

"I'll eat them on the way. Come on, Mama, please."

"All right. Help me clear the table, and then we'll go."

As they drove along, Christina told her mother about Pete, Ginger, and Kathy. "Pete has a burro, and his name is Frankie. Both he and Ginger live on the Indian reservation, and Ginger rides her father's pretty gray horse. Kathy lives near here, and she has the loveliest little mare, a real sorrel with a flaxen mane and tail. So her name is Flaxie. She got her for her birthday just before school was out. I've seen those kids at school but never knew them. They're going to help me look for Wallace if we don't find him at the pig place today. Oh, I hope he's there!"

"Don't worry so much. If he isn't there, he's somewhere else. I'm glad you've found some friends. Now where did the little boy say to turn when we get through town?"

When they reached the vicinity of the pig farm, Mrs. Wood said, "We didn't really need directions, did we? All we had to do was to follow our noses!"

"What an awful smell! Poor Wallace. For his sake he shouldn't be here, but, oh, I hope we find him here!"

"Don't be too disappointed if we don't. We'll find him somewhere."

When they got out of the car, Christina's mother said, "Goodness," and held her handkerchief to her nose.

This was not really a pig farm but a place where young pigs were brought in from wherever they could be purchased and fed garbage until they were heavy enough for market. All the pens and pigs were filthy, and the rotting garbage seemed to poison the air.

"Poor pigs!" exclaimed Christina.

Pigs of all sizes and colors came running to the fence, all talking at once. They always hoped that when they saw people, they might be fed something good.

Some of the spotted ones looked enough like Wallace to almost give Christina hope, at least to make her visualize him even more clearly, but plainly none was Wallace. The ones that resembled him only made her feel worse because of the familiar appearance.

She turned away sadly.

"Dear, are you sure?" her mother asked. "I see a dozen that look like your pig. At least, I think so. They're all so covered with dirt that it's hard to tell."

"Oh no, Mama, Wallace isn't here."

"Look carefully again. How can you tell so quickly?"

"Well, wouldn't you know me if you saw me in a whole penful of people? Even if I needed a bath?"

"I suppose you're right. Shall we drive through the alleys again and look in back yards before we go home?"

"Yes, let's."

But they saw no other pigs.

Chapter Seventeen

On the day that Wallace had been lost for a week, the air turned heavy and sultry. Beautiful thick white clouds pushed up over the mountains. By midmorning thunder began to roar and rumble. Flashes of lightning stabbed the clouds, and all at once the rain poured down.

For Wallace, the rain was a very good thing.

For an hour and a half, it poured down and made a delicious fragrance out of earth, sagebrush, and leaves. All the hollows in the rocks overflowed, and little streams ran and formed pools in low places. When the sun came out at last, the newly polished leaves and stones sparkled, and steam rose from the warm, wet earth.

Wallace kept moving farther and farther from his spring by the willow because now he could find a good drink of water almost anywhere.

The children rode again in the direction they had started that first day, keeping near to the canyon that twisted toward town.

"Golly," said Pete, "if the pig had been around here, the rain went and washed out his tracks, unless we can find some new ones where he's walked since the rain."

"But that would be good," said Christina, "because then we'd know where he'd been not long ago. All his tracks would be fresh."

"Well, keep looking."

They reached a brushy hill slope from which they could look down on the little town. It was a miserable place, hot and unshaded under the summer sun.

"Glad we aren't there," said Ginger.

"Glad we aren't there in school," Pete added. "I hate school."

Christina counted, "We've got some of July, all of August, and a few days of September. Oh, we've just got to find Wallace before then!"

"We will," Ginger promised.

Suddenly Christina shrieked. "Look!" She began calling desperately, "Wallace! Wallace, come here!"

"You seen him?" asked Pete eagerly, and then saw which way Christina was pointing. Hanging on a clump of sagebrush was the faded and frayed remains of Wallace's red, white, and blue ribbon.

"He's been here," exulted Christina, "he's been right here. He must be around somewhere!"

"But before the rain," Pete pointed out. "See, no tracks."

"He can't be far! Anyway, we know now that he must be safe here in the hills."

Kathy suggested, "Let's just keep circling. We might pick up new tracks."

Pete said, "It's my turn to ride Whitewing now."

Ginger obligingly jumped down.

Christina was always amazed at their good humor about whose turn it was to ride the gray. Children she knew at school would have most certainly been quarreling over the privilege. Just now, however, she was too excited over the possible nearness of Wallace to ponder about this.

"I always like Frankie," Ginger remarked.

"Like me and my pony." Christina sighed. "I love him dearly, but he's nearly too little for me. When I was little, I had to ride only in the home pastures. Now that I'm big and they'll let me ride anywhere, Button is too old to ride far."

"Your father has all those quarter horses. Why can't you ride one of them?" Kathy asked.

"Well, they won't let me. They're too busy putting a good rein on them. They've got to be perfect cutting horses. Anyway, I wouldn't want to have one to ride because they always get sold; and I'd just get to love one and he'd be the next one to go. So, I better stick to my pony. I can keep him. I keep hoping they'll get me a full-sized horse all my own. I don't even have a dog. Our old dog died, and we felt so bad, we couldn't get another. Maybe later we will. That's one reason I liked Wallace so much. He was my very own, like the pony. Oh, I hope we find him soon! I miss him so much."

Their circling took them to the spring by the willow, and Christina exclaimed joyfully, "Look, he's been here, too! See all the little places where he's rooted in the earth."

Pete pointed out, "He must of started traveling before the rain quit. I don't see no tracks."

"We might find some tracks further on, somewhere or other—wherever he was after the rain stopped. He can't be so very far away," Ginger suggested hopefully.

Christina kept calling, wishing hard that from somewhere her pig would run out of the brush.

But he was too far away to hear her.

Chapter Eighteen

W**ALLACE'S** wanderings had brought him to a narrow dirt road that led through a high stand of chaparral further back into the hills. The road brought him to a wooden gate, which sagged drearily on its hinges. Wallace crept under it and continued on his way. Soon he began to hear lively sounds— dogs barking, cows mooing, ducks quacking—and because he was lonely, the sounds interested him. Also he picked up some good grainy scents, and suddenly he was hungry for food other than the dry grass and rooty things that he had had to eat of late.

This was some sort of home place toward which his instincts led him. Though he had been forced to live like a wild animal, he was a domestic creature, and he liked companionship. He had known no pigs since he had left his first home, and he had no idea that he was a pig.

Around a bend of the road, he saw a building. He made a surprised sound to himself and stood still to observe what was there.

He didn't know that he was arriving at a remarkable place, the home of the Garb family. The Garbs' house, at which he was staring, was old, weathered, and sprawly. Once it had been elegant, with its veranda columns painted white and all its gingerbread scallopings also white. Now the white paint flaked, and the rest of it was a beaten orange-brown color.

It smelled good, like food and animals.

Wallace moved nearer. The sounds he heard were not coming from the house but from off to the side of the house where now he saw an enormous barn. An imaginative human might be able to discern that half a century ago the barn had been painted red, though of course Wallace didn't know or care.

Between the barn and the house sat five ancient automobiles, none of which would ever move again under its own power. But they made good sleeping places for dogs and cats, of which the Garbs had many.

With the exception of Mr. Garb, who was resting from a carpentry job he had been doing that day, the entire Garb family was over by the barn doing evening chores. This was a noisy occupation, with Garbs yelling at Garbs, goats and sheep bleating, cows impatient to be fed, calves bawling for milk. A horse nickered for his grain, and a mule brayed. There was a loud high sound of pig squealing, which somehow excited Wallace.

He was about to move cautiously nearer when he was sighted by several dogs, who instantly began to bark. Two little boys appeared to see what the barking was about.

"Look, Mama! A pig!"

"Don't chase him," yelled Mrs. Garb. "Freddie, Ernie, you come right back here. Don't scare him. Teensa, hurry, get me a bucket with some grain in it. Mebbe I can ketch him."

It was ridiculous to ask Teensa, who was nearly sixteen years old, to hurry. She was afraid that she might scuff the polish off her toe nails or shake her hair out of its elaborate arrangement. Her younger sister Doreen scurried ahead of her and got the bucket for her mother.

"Now you kids stay back," Mrs. Garb ordered. "You danged dogs shut up, get back there. Here, piggy, good piggy," and she shook the bucket so that Wallace could hear the grain rattle.

Ready to run, if need be, Wallace stood watching Mrs. Garb approach. He smelled the good rolled barley. Mrs. Garb, who was large, wore blue jeans, a torn blue work shirt, and a battered cowboy hat. To Wallace, she looked good, and she spoke now in a soft, kind voice and moved slowly. He even took two steps toward her. She set the bucket down, and unable to resist it, he hurried and grabbed as much as he could stuff into his mouth. Then he ran off a few steps and, eying Mrs. Garb, opened his mouth and dumped out the grain, as his mouthful was too large. He gulped it down in four bites and looked longingly at the bucket.

"Come, piggy, come," and Mrs. Garb picked up the bucket and backed away with it. Wallace followed.

She let him have three more helpings before she backed into a pen and, once Wallace was also inside, put down the bucket and yelled for someone to shut the gate, quick. Wallace finished the grain.

The children, except Teensa, who was above such matters, crowded around to look at their new pig. Mrs. Garb began rubbing him behind his ears, and Wallace flopped down, presenting his belly to be rubbed.

"Oh, Mama, ain't he cute? He's a pretty pig. He's a lot different-looking from Gerber and Hamlet."

Gerber and Hamlet, both big Tamworth pigs, were red-

dish brown with ears that stood perkily up, ears that had given them an adorable elfish look when they had been piglets. They had looked like little gnomes. Now they were both fastened on long chains because they had to be kept out of the way at feeding time, and they were screaming their heads off because no one had gotten around to feeding them yet.

First someone had given the Garbs Gerber because he was a tiny runt, about to die, and he had been cared for tenderly, bottle-fed, and allowed to live in the house until he grew so big that one day he nearly upset the cookstove. Next someone gave them Hamlet, also weak and small, and he had lived in the house until he had rooted most of the linoleum off the floor. Being unable to eat Gerber because of their affection for him, the Garbs had hoped that they might eat the second pig. They had named him Hamlet to remind themselves of how good ham tastes, but Hamlet had even more charm, if possible, than Gerber. It wasn't at all likely that the Garbs would eat him.

From time to time, Mr. Garb spoke disgustedly on the subject of keeping such worthless pigs and of how good pork is, but the truth was that he couldn't have swallowed a bite of either one of them.

Now, wondering what the commotion was about, he came out of the house and walked over to the barn. Unlike his wife, he was extremely thin and tall. His bib overalls hung loosely about his frame. He had taken off his shoes to rest his feet, and he hadn't bothered to put them back on. He stepped carefully.

"Look, Papa, we got a new pig!"

"Hmmm. Well. Fine-looking pig."

"Teensa," called Mrs. Garb, "run and get the pig a bucket

of water." She knew very well that Teensa never ran anywhere or got anything, but it wouldn't hurt to keep trying. Perhaps someday, if ordered about enough, the girl would snap out of this languid trance into which she had fallen.

Doreen came lugging a bucket of water, and Wallace drank gratefully.

"This pig now," said Mr. Garb, "we can eat him. He ain't a teensy pig being raised in the house on a bottle and all."

"Mebbe so," agreed Mrs. Garb.

"You kids don't pet him and play with him. Hear me?" their father ordered. "Go finish up the chores and leave this here pig alone."

In time everything quieted down. The old mule, whose name was Weaver, got his oats, and the horse, old Jeff, had his. Enough milk was secured from the three cows to supply the people part of the family. The calves were turned loose to take what was left and then penned again. Goats got milked, and kids were fed. The sheep and their big lambs were penned for the night. Grain was scattered for the chickens, ducks, and turkeys; Gerber and Hamlet, fed and quiet, were released from their chains.

The Garbs retired to the house to feed their dogs and cats and themselves. The chickens and turkeys flew up into trees. Only the ducks continued to wander about.

Left to himself, Wallace grew lonely again.

Chapter Nineteen

T HE pen in which Wallace was enclosed was in as bad repair as everything else on the Garb ranch, and it took only
the least bit of rooting and pushing before Wallace was free.
Making pleased noises to himself, he began to explore in the
vicinity of the barn. He was confronted at once with Gerber,
who was enormous, with huge yellowed tusks. Gerber told
him to get out, and he got.

When Hamlet had been a young pig and turned outdoors
for the first time, Gerber hadn't liked him either and would
make savage rushes at him. Hamlet would scream and run
under the house and hide, refusing to come out.

After a while, however, Gerber grew accustomed to having Hamlet around, and by the time Hamlet was grown,
they were friends, except when one or the other found
something good to eat.

Hamlet, having forgotten how he felt when Gerber used
to be mean to him, now had no hospitable feelings toward
Wallace. As soon as he saw him, he ran at him. Wallace ut-
tered a terrified shriek and got out of the way. Neither of
the big pigs pursued the matter further. The evening was
too warm to give chase. All they wanted was that the in-
truder stay away from them.

Wallace wandered into the midst of the ducks, and they

quacked and tripped over their feet as they scurried out of his way. Then he decided to find the people, and he trotted toward the Garb back door, making pleasant remarks.

The Garbs were gathered around the dinner table. "What's that?" said Mrs. Garb.

Freddie went to look and reported, "The new pig's on the back porch shoving at the door."

"Don't let him in," Mr. Garb ordered.

"Here, Teensa," said Mrs. Garb, "you take some potato peelings and coax him back to the pen and shut him up and fix where he got out."

Teensa merely stopped chewing and gave her mother a scathing look.

"You didn't help one bit with the chores, Teensa. Time you did something. You're as useless as a toad's hind pocket."

Teensa shrugged and went on eating.

"Doreen?"

"Oh, Ma! I did most of the work!" But Doreen took the table scraps and went out.

"Ca-ca-ca!" Wallace said in his affectionate, whispering voice, happy to see a friendly human. Very willingly he followed Doreen back and into his pen, and as he gobbled his potato peelings, she found a piece of baling wire and some-what mended the hole he had made.

By the time she was at table again, Wallace had arrived at the back door.

"Oh, Ma! Might as well leave him be. He won't go away."

"You couldn't of fixed that pen very good."

"Well, it's nearly dark, and I done what I could. He won't run away, Ma. Nothing ever runs away from here."

"I wish I could," Teensa remarked.

"Miss Hoity Toity, just you wait until you get out in the world. You'll wish you was back here all safe. Kids don't appreciate what they got any more."

Teensa was indeed a trial. When she had been younger, she had been as good as gold, but now that she considered herself to be almost grown, she had suddenly become difficult. She lay around reading about movie stars. She detested the ramshackle house, the animals, her uncouth family, and she wished for beautiful clothes and handsome boy friends.

Doreen, at eleven, was a scrawny freckled-faced child, eager to please and fond of all creatures. Freddie, nine, and Ernie, eight, had freckles, too, and pale hair and light eyes. They were good little boys, and their mother sighed, wondering if all of them would get silly when they reached Teensa's age.

Since it was clear that no one was going to let him come into the house and since the only attention he received was a sudden kick from Teensa when he had started shrieking and pushing on the door, Wallace settled down to spend the night on the back porch. It was nearly as pleasant as being in the house.

He awakened to hear the domestic sounds of roosters crowing and the fluttering sounds of poultry descending from trees. The ducks were already walking around and quacking. Gerber and Hamlet were fond of sleeping late, and only one of them had gotten around to opening one eye.

Wallace walked down the porch steps and nosed about but found nothing worth eating. Presently he heard the Garbs stirring, and then he smelled their breakfast cooking. This made him so hungry that he began to yell.

Mr. Garb had to be gotten off to work when he'd rather

stay home and rest. But the Garbs always owed a lot of bills, and of course they made no money off their land, so Mr. Garb was a handyman, carpenter, and odd-job doer.

After Mr. Garb had climbed into his old red truck and argued with it a while to get it going, he went roaring off, and the rest of the family headed for the barn.

Wallace was delighted to see them all, even Teensa. Pigs are forgiving animals.

The first chore always was to put Gerber and Hamlet on their chains. To this the pigs submitted willingly, because they were aware that they wouldn't get fed unless they were chained. If someone forgot to chain them and opened the door into the feed room, they dove right in and began creating havoc, tearing open feed sacks and resisting being ousted.

Wallace, happily at large, nosed into the feed room and was kicked by Teensa. He protested loudly. "Find him a chain, somebody," Mrs. Garb yelled. "We can't get anything done with him running around."

"There ain't no more chains," Doreen told her.

"Well, find some kind of rope, then."

One of the boys produced a somewhat frayed rope, and Mrs. Garb tied it around Wallace's neck. "He's used to being tied up," she observed as she fastened the rope's other end to a fence post.

"Wonder where he came from, Ma?"

"Dunno. But he's nice and tame."

If someone had come around looking for a stray pig, the Garbs, who were honest, would not have tried to keep Wallace. The Garbs had heard nothing of a runaway pig because they were too absorbed in the excitement of life at home to go around talking with people. Mr. Garb seldom paid any attention to what anyone said to him. It took all his powers of concentration to do any task that the day demanded. Teensa got around more, but if she heard anything about a lost pig, she paid no attention. She couldn't care less about the subject, anyway.

Doreen asked, "What should we name him, Ma?"

"We better not name him anything. Your paw's determined we're going to eat him as soon as cold weather comes. Best not to name anything you're gonna eat."

"I'll call him Piggy," Doreen decided. "That's not really exactly a name."

Doreen came with grain and hay, and after Wallace had eaten, he lay down with his front hoofs stretched out before him and watched what was going on.

"Now," suggested Mrs. Garb, when all the feeding and milking was done, "we'd best always remember to turn the big pigs loose last. Always untie the new one first because they might pick on him when he's tied up."

Turned free, Wallace accompanied his friends as far as the back door. He was beginning to like his new home.

Chapter Twenty

Dogs and cats were always going in and out of the house, and Wallace didn't understand why he couldn't, too. He did manage once to squeeze through into the kitchen when a dog was let in, but Teensa booted him out before he had a chance to look around.

The Garbs had never intended to possess so many dogs and cats, but when puppies and kittens were born, what could they do? They gave away what they could, but always there are more kittens and puppies than there are people who want them.

To add to their troubles, everyone for miles around knew how soft-hearted the Garbs were, so that many an unwanted dog and cat had been abandoned on the Garb road. Naturally, they found their way to the house, as had Wallace, and naturally they couldn't be allowed to starve, so of course they didn't go away. Mr. Garb was also inclined to pick up any very lost-looking dog he found wandering the highway, for he was afraid that it might get run over.

Every day Mrs. Garb cooked up a big cauldron of corn meal mixed with table scraps, and every evening each dog and cat got fed a goodly portion, and on this fare they all flourished.

Scraps unsuitable to go into the corn-meal pot—water-melon rinds, cucumber peelings, and the like—were tossed out the back door and soon dispatched by pigs and poultry.

Poor as the Garbs might be, nothing went very hungry on their place.

The dogs, sixteen in number at that time, ranged in size and age from toddling puppies on up. Short dogs, long dogs, tall dogs, small dogs, dogs of every color and shape—they had one thing in common, they were happy dogs.

Wallace settled down under a shade tree in the side yard. A friendly cat came and rubbed against him and purred. A puppy came and barked at him and then wanted to play with his long ears. Its sharp, small teeth made him squeal. He swung his head sideways and gave the puppy a good bump, which scared it so that it yipped and ran to find its mother.

"I wish you kids would get out and clean up the yard," said Mrs. Garb. "You haven't got at it for a long time now, and all those cans and papers will blow to kingdom come, once the east winds start. There ain't a one of you doing anything. You, too, Teensa."

Teensa was the only one who grumbled loudly, which was funny, as she was the one who complained about the way the place looked.

Keeping a wary eye open for the big pigs, Wallace accompanied the children to the barn, where they each got an empty feed sack for collecting debris. Wallace decided that he liked Doreen best, and he stayed close to her. He nosed around near her as she picked up cans and papers, and he made remarks. From time to time Doreen would stop work and pet him a little, which pleased him.

Most of the dogs found that this was an interesting occupation, too. There were old bones that they wanted to salvage now that their attention had been brought to them. The oldest dog, Scrapper, kept his eye on one corner of the yard, where he had some treasures buried by a stump. He knew exactly where he kept four bones and a piece of old harness leather, which, from time to time, he liked to exhume and chew.

This yard-cleaning business was making him nervous.

When one of his grown sons went over and began sniffing around where Scrapper's property was hidden, the old dog's hackles went straight up, and walking on stiff legs, he moved to threaten his son.

The younger dog snarled back, and suddenly the two of them were at it, screaming and fighting. The excitement was too much to allow some of the other dogs to be mere observers. In another second there was a noisy free-for-all going on. An old yellow bobtailed tom cat, big and powerful, flung himself into the fray, and fur flew in all directions.

The children jumped up and down and yelled while Wallace quivered with excitement. A pig is easily stirred by an uproar.

Mrs. Garb stood on the back porch and began screaming for Hamlet and Gerber, which was unnecessary as they were already on the way, loping at top speed. From their napping spot on the shady side of the barn, they had heard the commotion, which roused them immediately.

Nothing ever was so stimulating to Gerber and Hamlet as the sound of a dog fight, and banging their heads from side to side, knocking dogs helter-skelter, they dove into the melee.

Wallace, desiring to be in the thick of things, dared not because of his fear of the big pigs. He had to content himself by running in circles and shrieking.

The fight was over almost instantly. Dogs departed in various directions, and the old tom cat sailed up a tree. Still excited, puffing and snorting and breathing hard, the big pigs retired to the nearest shade. Not wanting to attract their attention, Wallace quieted at once.

"Those are the best pigs," said Mrs. Garb complacently. "They allus stop dog fights. Them and the old tom cat. Now you kids get back to work. Pick up all that stuffing the pups pulled from the old sofa, too. We'll have a dandy bonfire after a while. There's not a stir of wind, and it'll be safe."

This inspired the children. Even Teensa began to take a slight interest in her occupation. When all the trash had been collected and dumped in one place, there was an imposing amount of it.

Mrs. Garb struck a match, and everyone stood back to enjoy the motion and colors of flames and the thick smoke that billowed straight up toward the sky.

"Fire! Fire!" Ernie and Freddie yelled joyfully, and went dancing as they thought Indians danced, around and around the fire. Doreen ran looking for sticks to throw on to keep it burning, and Teensa sat down on the back-porch steps to enjoy it.

Wallace backed away. The day was hot enough without a fire.

Suddenly they all became aware of a new sound.

Siren screaming, a red forestry truck came flashing up the road.

"Lookee!" yelled the little boys, and ran toward the truck as it huffed to a halt.

Teensa, careful not to show any hurry, removed herself from the porch steps and sauntered into view. There were five forestry boys on the truck, and four of them began climbing down and drifting in the direction of Teensa. She regarded them through her eyelashes and approved of the look of them in their neat uniforms.

The driver, older than the others, took a notebook from his pocket and approached. Mrs. Garb had vanished into the house.

"Are your parents home?" he asked politely.

"Mama's in the house," Freddie said, and both little boys began calling, "Ma! Ma! Come out. The man wants to see you!"

Mrs. Garb had to emerge. She did so reluctantly, having a strong feeling that this was not a social call. Doreen hovered behind her.

"Ma'am, what is all this?" the official-appearing young man asked softly.

"We was just burning some trash."

"But, ma'am, all trash burning must be done before the hour of 8 A.M. and after the hour of 8 P.M."

"So what's the difference? It's all bare and clear where we're burning. There ain't no wind. We had to get rid of this trash. 'Twas a fire hazard," she added righteously.

"There's a big difference," he explained. "The man on the lookout sees smoke at trash-burning time, and he knows what it is. If everyone was to burn at any hour, there'd be smokes all day long, and the trucks would have to investigate each one. Costs taxpayers' money every time we go out."

"So that's great. Our house could burn down at trash-burning time, and no one would come to fight the fire. They'd just say it was trash. Maybe you think it is, but it's our home."

"Nonetheless, it's the law. There's a fine and a possible

jail sentence for burning at odd hours without a permit."

At this Freddie and Ernie stopped admiring the red truck and began to cry. Teensa, who detested them, put her arms around them and drew them close to her. She was a heroine, defending her little brothers from the Gestapo. The forestry boys observed this with admiration.

Doreen began to cry softly. Wallace came to see what was going on and said, "Erful."

One of the boys put down a hand and petted Wallace. "Nice pig," he observed.

Mrs. Garb wiped away an invisible tear. "Poor little feller. What's to become of him and all the critters, and our poor children? We got no money for paying any fine."

Freddie and Ernie howled louder.

"Shame on you, scaring little children."

"But, ma'am, all I said was. . . . Ma'am, this is only a warning. Listen, ma'am, honest, I'm not going to turn you in, not this time. Just don't go to burning trash at the wrong hours. Please."

Even Teensa looked ready to weep and might have squeezed out a few tears if it hadn't been that it would do damage to her eye make-up.

"Come on, lady, cheer up. I just said it was only a warning. Oh, come on, boys, let's get out of here."

One was a little slower to climb back onto the truck. He lingered, saying some comforting words to Teensa.

The little boys left off crying and started admiring the truck again. It was too bad that when it left, it did not make its siren go. But all the forestry boys waved good-by to Teensa.

Mrs. Garb watched the dust cloud disappear down the

road. She sighed. "A body can't call their soul their own any more."

Teensa was pleased with developments. She was going to the movies Saturday night with that forestry boy.

Chapter Twenty-one

Wherever the children went, Wallace followed. Doreen and her brothers weren't very active during the heat of the day. Most of their time was spent under trees. Doreen had her own playhouse where a pepper tree's heavy branches bent to the ground and provided green walls. Ernie and Freddie didn't like playing house, but sometimes they did for lack of anything more interesting to do.

In her pepper-tree house, Doreen kept her doll buggy and her two dolls left over from her younger days. They had ceased to be pretty dolls. One had been scalped, and one had a broken nose ever since they had been victims in an Indian massacre when Freddie and Ernie were Indians.

They wanted to play at being forestry boys now and were constructing a fire road in the dust under an oak tree, brushing away the dry brittle leaves, making a track on which they could push their tiny toy cars. They made sounds like sirens as they rushed imaginary trucks to imaginary fires.

They bored Doreen, and with Wallace at her heels, she crept into her leafy playhouse. Inside, it looked pleasant and cool. Light filtered greenly through the fernlike leaves. It smelled all sharp and peppery.

Doreen decided that the pig would be very good to play house with. She could pretend that he was her little boy.

Piggy didn't seem to be a fitting name for one's child, but since she wasn't allowed to give him a real name, he'd have to be Piggy.

Perhaps he could learn to mind a little, and as he went rooting about exploring the earth, she said to him, "Now you sit down and be a good little boy. Mother's got to be busy. Sit down."

To her surprise he did. "My, what a good little fellow," she told him. "Can you shake hands like a polite little boy?"

Daintily Wallace handed her a cloven hoof.

"For goodness' sake!" Doreen exclaimed. She tried it again. "Shake hands," and the pig did.

"Well, I never!" She stared at him in wonderment. "You're certainly lots smarter than old Gerber and Hamlet. Maybe I can learn you something else. Now you better lie down and go to sleep. Time for your nap. Lie down now."

Wallace obediently went down. "Why, you're just a darling pig! You learn so fast." She petted his belly, and he groaned with pleasure.

"You can almost sing. Maybe I can learn you to sing." And she began humming to accompany his happy pig sounds. "Well you take a nap now, and then we'll have tea."

Her cupboard was a wooden packing box in which she kept the broken remains of a set of doll dishes. She hadn't looked at them for some time, and she was dismayed at how many more were broken. "The boys must 've got into them," she decided as she searched for some tiny unbroken cups.

A wooden fruit crate, turned upside down, served as a table, and its cloth was a dish towel once salvaged from the kitchen. Doreen set her table and thought how cute the pig would look, sitting at the table.

"Come on," she told him. "Come sit here."

By now he was sleeping soundly in his comfortable spot. Doreen peered at him, noticing the way his mouth was constructed, so that he wore two smiles on each side of his face. She tickled him under the chin. "Come now, tea is ready."

Wallace roused and grunted sleepily. "Come on. You have to sit down at the table."

Lazily he stood up and followed her, and she made him sit in his place. Doreen giggled with joy. "You look so cute."

She took an imaginery sip from her small cup and gave him one from his.

"He ought to wear a bib," she thought, "and wouldn't he look cute in a bonnet! Why, I could dress him up," she decided, "like a real little boy."

She hurried to the house, where no one paid any attention to her. Wallace followed her halfway and climbed onto the discarded sofa that sat on the shady side of the building. Doreen soon returned with a bundle partly concealed under her blouse, coaxed Wallace off the sofa, and took him back to her playhouse.

He didn't seem to mind as she stuffed him into a pair of Freddie's jeans. She had to roll the pants legs up. Otherwise, the fit was nearly perfect, though she regretted that she hadn't brought scissors with which to cut a hole for his tail. The blue cotton shirt she had found went very well across his shoulders. She buttoned it up the front and rolled up the sleeves. One of Teensa's scarfs went over his head and tied under his chin.

Doreen hugged her little boy pig. "What a darling child you are! Now that you are all dressed up, let's take your little sisters for a ride in the baby buggy."

When she had shoved the buggy out from under the tree and started pushing it toward the house, Wallace made a surprised sound of pleasure, as though he had recognized a friend. Then he came along and gave the handle a shove with his snout.

"Well I swan," said Doreen. "You can push your little sisters all yourself." As she approached the house, she yelled, "Ma, Ma, come look what Piggy's doing!"

Mrs. Garb was too astonished at what the pig was doing to be angry because her son's garments had been borrowed. She stood laughing until she wept real tears this time.

But Teensa was furious. "My very best scarf on a dirty old pig!"

Chapter Twenty-two

M R. Garb wasn't pleased either when he heard about the pig wearing clothes and pushing the doll buggy. "I told the kids to leave him alone. We're gonna eat him, come cool weather. Food costs money, and I ain't a gonna let any more good pork go to waste."

"But, Pa," Doreen protested, "Piggy follows me around no matter whether I call him or not. Isn't my fault."

"Shut him in the pen, then."

"He won't stay."

"Fix it so's he will. Tomorrow. All you kids get out there and you mend that pigpen. And then you keep the pig in it. Hear?"

"Yes, Pa."

"It ain't as if he was one we raised. He's a stranger. This pig's a stranger, and we'll eat him."

Alas, the polka-dot pig was no stranger to Doreen, and she loved him dearly. She sighed sorrowfully.

The next morning, without any enthusiasm, Doreen and her brothers set to work. Teensa sat in the shade and watched for a while, then drifted back to the house.

Her brothers and sister got some haywire from the feed barn and started weaving it into the hog wire, pulling together what had been pig-sized holes. Wallace stayed with them as if interested in what they were doing for him.

He wasn't interested, though, when after a long time they completed the job and shut him in with a reward of some grain. Doreen placed a bucket of water for him. It wasn't a bad pen, for one tree dropped shade into it.

In a second Wallace gobbled his grain, noticed that he was not only deserted but confined, and began to protest. His screams rose higher and higher, grew louder and louder, reached a piercing crescendo. Gerber and Hamlet, excited by the noise, came hurrying, and Wallace was terrified lest they get in and bite him.

The day was too warm for the pigs to go to all that trouble, and having discovered what the noise was about, they settled down to some more sleeping.

Wallace settled down to the not very difficult task of working his way out.

When Mr. Garb came home from work, there was the new pig sleeping very comfortably on the sofa by the side of the house.

"I told you kids . . ." he started, and the children interrupted.

"But we did, Pa. We fixed up the pen and put him into it. And he got right out. So Ma made us fix the place he got out of, and he got out again."

"That's so." Mrs. Garb backed them up. "The kids was really busy with that pigpen."

"Kids don't know how to work these days. Tomorrow I got no job anywhere, so I'll just fix a pen that pig will stay in."

And he thought he did. It took Wallace an hour or so to find the best place to root a hole and crawl out under. When next Mr. Garb saw him, the pig was reclining in his favorite spot, the sofa with the stuffing spilling out. He looked regal, like a Roman after a banquet.

"See, Pa?" Doreen said.

"Never mind. I'll fix a place yet that he won't get out of."

But the more Mr. Garb worked, the more expert Wallace became as an escape artist. Mr. Garb never consciously gave up, but he didn't get around to constructing a tighter pen, though he planned to.

In the meantime, life went on as usual for Wallace. He spent much of his day with Doreen and was tied up only at feeding times. If it weren't for Gerber and Hamlet roaming at large, Wallace wouldn't have needed a pen. He could have stayed tied. But he couldn't be left tied while the others were loose to attack him, and this was to his advantage.

Doreen tried very hard and very unsuccessfully to ignore him. Then she began trying to think of some way to save him. Perhaps she could hide him somewhere out in the brush, or perhaps she ought to leave home and run away with her pig.

When she considered further, neither plan was practical. If he were hidden, he would have to be tied, and left to himself, he was sure to scream bloody murder and everyone would hear where he was. If the two ran away together, where could they go?

Only Wallace was unworried. Life was pleasant for him.

Chapter Twenty-three

Besides Doreen, Wallace found another friend. This was a tall black Nubian goat, a wether, of no use or importance except that he was a pet. Like Gerber and Hamlet, he had been raised in the house because he had been one of a set of triplets and extra weak. The Garbs seemed to have made an unspoken law—they couldn't bring themselves to eat or sell any animal that had been brought up in the house.

So the goat, Billy, scampered about with the children and spent part of his time with the other goats and part of his time near the house with the people. He grew to enormous size.

Goats are as curious as they are intelligent, and when he kept seeing Wallace, he grew interested. One day he inspected him closer. Wallace looked up at the black creature looming high above him and didn't know whether or not to feel alarmed. But the goat sniffed him gently at first, and Wallace became reassured.

He grunted some conversation at the goat. The goat thought that this was funny. It inspired him to rear high, turn his body slightly to the side, and give Wallace a playful poke with his horns as he came down. Wallace understood at once, as animals do, what was meant to be a playful gesture. Billy danced away and came back at Wallace. Wallace bounced in a circle; Billy spun in a circle.

Doreen watched them and stood laughing. It delighted her to see animals of two different kinds playing together. "Look, Mama," Doreen called.

Her mother enjoyed this, too. "Well that's good. Let him be Billy's friend instead of yours. Your pa doesn't want you to make a pet out of him."

"Oh, Ma," Doreen said sadly.

"Can't be helped. Your pa's determined."

"But Billy would miss him, too."

"Billy has lots of other friends."

Doreen sighed and wished that she could think of some way to make life safe for her pig.

Usually it was in the early morning or in the cool of the evening that the pig and the goat played. During the warm hours each was inclined to sleep. Sometimes they slept near each other in the shade. Sometimes Billy wandered off with the other goats to climb rocks and to nibble the brush.

Doreen observed that a goat has one way of playing and a pig another. Goats like to get forehead to forehead with one another and push, though there are many variations in their play. A pig plays at fighting by swinging his head sideways, because a grown pig has tusks on each side, and the sideways attack is so that the sharp tusks can rip the enemy.

When Billy caught the pig squarely, pressing hard with the curved part of his horns, there was nothing else for Wallace to do but to brace his feet and push back with his forehead as a goat or a ram would do. He was learning a goat's way of playing. It is natural for a goat also to swing his head and deliver a glancing bump, much as a pig would do. Each one's way of playing fitted the other's, except that Wallace couldn't possibly stand on his hind legs as Billy did so gracefully.

Doreen said to her brothers, "I bet that Piggy thinks he has horns, just like the goat. I bet he's gonna be awful surprised one day to find he hasn't got hard things on his head. I never seen a pig play like a goat before."

Ernie considered this. "I bet the pig doesn't know what he looks like. Did he ever see himself, I wonder?"

"Maybe in a pool somewheres if he was getting a drink. I hadn't thought about that. He probably doesn't really know what himself looks like. He ought to see that he ain't got horns because if ever he was in a real fight and counting on horns he don't have, he'd be in a fix."

"We ought to show him."

"Teensa's got that hand mirror she keeps in her room and looks at all the time. Where is Teensa? Freddie, you could sneak in and get it. Hide it under your shirt."

"Teensa's on the porch reading a movie book," Ernie reported. "Freddie, you sneak in the house through the kitchen."

Freddie giggled and complied. It was getting near chore time. The late afternoon was cooling, and the animals were all near the barn. The three children hurried over, Freddie tenderly carrying Teensa's treasure inside his shirt. It was a fancy mirror, handle and back decorated with pink and gold inlay.

They found Billy and Wallace together, rather languidly poking each other about. They were waiting for time to be fed. They regarded the children cheerfully. Their arrival must mean that food was soon to be served.

"Look, Piggy," Freddie said, pulling out the mirror. "Look at this, Piggy."

"Here, let me," said Ernie, and grabbed the mirror.

"No. I'm the one that got it."

"And I'm the one that thought of it," said Doreen, and seized it. "Now, Piggy, you look at you and you look at Billy, and, Billy, you look at you, too. See, Piggy, no horns."

First Wallace thought that they were offering him something to eat, and his snout smeared the bright glass. Doreen wiped it on her jeans. "No, Piggy, look—don't touch."

Billy wanted to see what this was and pushed Wallace away. Wallace whammed Billy. The children began to laugh. Wallace swung his head sharply. The mirror was knocked from Doreen's hand to land on a stone and drop into a thousand pieces.

"Oh!" The children groaned in dismay.

"What'll we do now?"

"Fix it."

"Can't."

"Hide it."

"Where?"

"Bury it."

"What'll Teensa say?"

"Plenty."

"She won't know."

"Oh yes, she will!" And there was Teensa right behind them, looking ready to murder all three. This was the first time she'd ever gone to the barn the minute her mother had told her to come help with chores.

"Ma, Ma," she sobbed. "Look what the kids did. Took my mirror and busted it. My beautiful, beautiful hand glass! I'll beat them to death."

"Go ahead," said Mrs. Garb reasonably. "They got it coming."

Mrs. Garb admired the way Teensa went into action. She, who exerted herself as little as possible and then unwillingly, now displayed speed, energy, and strength. "Shows what a body can do when they put their mind to it," Mrs. Garb observed.

The three tried fighting back, and they tried running away, but Teensa was like several wildcats at once. She had them subdued and howling before her mother said, "That's enough, Teensa. You can't murder them all the way. We can't afford funerals. Stop slapping them around now."

Exhausted, Teensa sat down to enjoy listening to the howls of anguish. She felt better. "That was quite a job," she remarked proudly. "Ma, how'd I ever have all that strength?"

"There's stuff in you that does it. When you get scared enough or mad enough, you get all this power. It's valuable when used right." Mrs. Garb added wisely, "It's good that you've learned about it."

The commotion had excited the pigs, but even Gerber and Hamlet were afraid to dive into this fray. Dog fights were one thing and people fights another. Wallace discreetly retired to the background. He never knew when a big pig was going to make a run at him.

Freddie sobbed, "Blasted pig. All his fault."

"He's the one busted it," Ernie shrieked. "I don't like him no more."

"I do," maintained Doreen.

"Well, let's get the chores done," said Mrs. Garb. "Come on, Freddie, Ernie. You ain't that all killed. Go chain the pigs."

Ernie started around the side of the barn and began to yell. "Ma! Here's a rattlesnake!"

"Get the long-handled hoe! No, wait. Let's see first what the new pig will do. Maybe *he* kills snakes like pigs are supposed to. Doreen, you call him around there, but don't you get too close."

"I don't want to. What if he gets bitten?"

" 'Twouldn't hurt him. Hogs got thick hides and layers of tallow underneath. Hurry up before it gets away."

The snake had not yet coiled and rattled. He was merely resting, stretched out in the shade.

Wallace saw him, shrieked, and ran.

"Well I never," said Mrs. Garb disgustedly. "You always hear how pigs kill rattlers, and both Gerber and Hamlet squeal and run, like an old woman seeing a mouse. And this pig's just as bad. I have yet to see a hog kill a snake. Hey, where's that hoe?" for now the snake sprang into a coil and rattled vigorously.

The children were awed. "Ain't he big?"

Their mother soon dispatched him.

"Oh, dear," Doreen thought. "If only Piggy had killed him. If only Piggy could do something right, then Pa might let me keep him."

This had been a very bad day.

Chapter Twenty-four

A T least Christina's searching for Wallace was no longer a lonely business. Her friends were as eager as she to find her pet, and the four of them spent days together.

Christina was curious about Ginger's home on the Indian reservation. "Is it nice there?" she asked.

"Oh, yes. Haven't you ever been on the reservation? Why don't you come see where I live," Ginger invited. "I have a pet deer."

"I'd like to—as soon as we find Wallace. I've never seen a tame deer."

"He's getting big," Kathy said.

"Where'd you get him?"

"We found him under a bush. You aren't supposed to touch little fawns because their mothers hide them and come back to feed them. But this one hadn't been fed. He was nearly starved. Something must have happened to his mother. So we took him and fed him goat's milk out of a baby bottle, and I guess he still thinks I'm his mother. He was so weak at first, we thought he'd die for sure."

"Oh, I wish I had known you kids sooner," Christina lamented.

"If it weren't for your lost pig, we never would have become friends," Kathy pointed out.

"That's so. I wish Wallace weren't lost, but since he is,

this summer is certainly different from most summers. Only we've just *got* to find Wallace pretty soon."

Christina's parents had met her friends when they had all ridden over one morning.

Her mother was glad that Christina was not riding around in the hills alone. Not that there was anything that could harm her if she remembered to be careful about rattlesnakes. Still, it was better that she had companions. And it was good that at last Christina was knowing other children.

Christina's father said, "With all of you looking, you'll surely find that pig one of these days."

But it was beginning to seem hopeless. They searched and searched in the vicinity of the spring where they knew that Wallace had once been. They rode further away from there and still found no tracks.

Late in the afternoon they came across the road Wallace had followed to Garbs'. None of his tracks were left in the dust. Too many cars had been over.

Pete said, "I know where this road goes. I think they have some pigs. Maybe he went there."

"How far is it?" Christina wanted to know. "Can we go there now or is it too late?"

Ginger looked at the lowering sun. "It won't be dark for a while yet. Maybe we could. Still, that would make us get home awful late, and Mama might be mad."

"It's quite a ways in to where they live," Pete said. "Maybe we ought to head straight for there first thing in the morning."

That same evening as the Garbs were eating supper, Mrs. Garb suddenly remembered something. "We forgot to turn those pigs loose. Teensa, you run out and undo them."

Teensa sighed wearily.

"Teensa, you never do one single thing I tell you to. Now git."

Her father said, "Teensa, mind your ma."

Teensa suggested, "Let one of the boys go."

"You never do nothing," Doreen told her.

"Teensa!" her father said firmly.

Sadly Teensa stood up and sauntered over to the barn. She unsnapped Hamlet's chain because she came to him first. She unsnapped Gerber's chain and gave him a kick to inform him that he was loose. Then she started to go untie Wallace.

Wallace made the mistake of his life. Seeing that the big pigs were loose while he was still tied and observing that Hamlet was moving in his direction, Wallace began to scream. Had he kept his mouth shut, his predicament might not have been noticed.

His shrieks excited Gerber and Hamlet, and they rushed at him. Terrified, Wallace bounced to the end of his rope and back again, pulling with all his might.

The rope snapped, and hotly pursued for a few yards, Wallace left the Garb ranch forever. He plunged into thick brush and kept right on going.

Teensa watched his departure without much interest.

Chapter Twenty-five

"Whatt was all the racket about?" Mrs. Garb wanted to know when Teensa returned to finish her supper.

"Oh, Ma. You know pigs. Always screeching about something."

In the morning Wallace was nowhere to be seen. Doreen called, "Piggy, Piggy, come, Piggy," but no polka-dot pig came trotting, eager for breakfast.

"Where is he at anyway?" Mrs. Garb asked. "Teensa, which way was he going last you seen him?"

"How'd I know?"

"Well, after we finish the chores, we'll have to look for him. Your pa will be put out if he's gone. He's been counting on some fresh pork."

Doreen stopped worrying at once. It occurred to her that she was glad that Piggy had run away. Certainly she didn't want to eat any of him.

She and the boys wandered around and saw where his tracks had disappeared into thick brush. "I don't want to crawl into there. Too snakey." Her brothers agreed.

Mrs. Garb suggested, "Why don't you kids get on Weaver and old Jeff and ride around where you can? Maybe if you ride down the road, you'll come to where he's run out of the brush, and you can follow his tracks."

"I get to ride Weaver, then," Doreen insisted. The mule

always traveled more willingly than the horse. Jeff had started to feel the burden of his years long before the mule had, though the mule was equally old.

As Christina and her friends were riding up the Garb road, they met Doreen and Ernie and Freddie. All animal ears went upright at once, and everyone stopped moving to stare. Frankie, the burro, was especially interested in the mule, who looked very strange to him. Jeff and Weaver had lived long enough to have seen all kinds of animals, so they were not surprised at the burro or the others, but they enjoyed looking at them.

Christina wasted no time. "We're hunting for a pig. A spotted one, about half grown or a little more. You haven't seen him, have you?"

"Why, that's funny," said Doreen. "We're looking for a pig, too. And he's spotted. A very nice pig. I was learning him to do tricks, and now he's run away."

"That sounds exactly like my pig. Where'd you get yours?"

"He just wandered in here. Well, maybe he is your pig. Oh, I hope he is your pig. I bet you wouldn't let anyone eat him."

"Oh, no! He's a bright trained pig."

"He is? And I thought I was learning him to sit down and shake hands and push a doll buggy and everything. You mean you'd already learned him all that?"

Christina nodded. "And I want so much to find him."

"Oh, I hope you do. I'll help you look."

"Where'd he take off from?" Pete wanted to know. "We could pick up his tracks and follow from there."

"How long ago did he run away?" Ginger asked.

"Last night, I guess. So he can't be gone too far. Let's ride back, and I'll show you where his tracks went into the brush."

"Oh, boy!" said Christina joyfully. "I bet we can find him this very day. He must be right around. Come on, Button, hurry!"

The whole cavalcade came jogging into the Garb front yard, where dogs barked enthusiastically. "Oh, look!" cried Christina. "What darling puppies!" Three fluffy small pups were making as much noise as their elders.

Mrs. Garb hurried out to see what the commotion was about. "Ma, oh, Ma," called Doreen. "We found out who Piggy belongs to. He belongs to this girl, and we're gonna find him for her. Now Pa can't eat him, can he?"

Mrs. Garb felt as pleased as Doreen. "Of course Pa wouldn't want to eat no pig that didn't belong to him. You kids look awful hot and thirsty. Get off and drink some water."

Christina was already off. She had seized a squirming pup that was whimpering and snuffling and licking her face. "Oh, I wish I could have him!"

"You can!" said Mrs. Garb delightedly.

"I'd have to ask my mother first, and probably I shouldn't take him until we find my pig. I wouldn't have time to take care of him. Will you save him for me?"

"You bet!" Mrs. Garb was glad to see people other than her own family, which sometimes she considered tiresome. "You kids rest a while, then look for the pig."

Christina sat down in the shade and cuddled her puppy. "Wonder what I'll name him. Oh, I hope I can have him!"

Doreen asked, "What's the pig's real name? I just called him Piggy."

"Wallace. The lady who had him first named him that. And he knows it's his name." Christina stood up. "I want to start looking for him right away."

"I'll show you where his tracks took off into the brush. It's real thick there, and I don't see how we can ride through it. And it looks snakey." Doreen walked, leading Weaver. "See, here's where he went."

Pete stared at the tracks and peered into the forest of brush. "By golly, I think me and Frankie could get through there. My burro can go anywhere. I'll go ahead and sort of break trail."

Christina carried the puppy back to the door yard and put him down. He didn't want to stay. He started waddling after her as she walked, leading Button, and she picked him up and carried him back again. "He does think he's mine."

"I'll hold him until you get out of sight," Mrs. Garb offered. "Now you children be careful about snakes. Stay up on your animals while you're in the brush."

Christina watched admiringly as Doreen climbed back on the big mule. Doreen had a system. While Weaver waited patiently, Doreen shinnied up his front leg.

Pete on his burro went first. The little boys followed on big Jeff, who was the right size to break trail. The rest strung out single file. They moved very slowly.

Pete was finding it difficult to follow pig tracks through the brush. Tiny dry leaves of scrub oak lay on the ground.

Finally he stopped. "I think he headed back for that spring. We ought to push our way out to the road and then go over to the spring. We might find his tracks crossing the road further along than where we came in at."

This seemed to be a sensible plan. All the children were scratched from riding in the brush, and it was extra hot and airless in the thickets. Once they fought their way out to the road, the going would be swifter, and they were all sure that they'd find Wallace near the spring.

Christina was the happiest she'd been since Wallace had disappeared. Soon he would be hers again, and then there was the puppy, which she was sure she'd be allowed to keep. And besides, she had all these good friends. She had liked Doreen at once. Doreen had seemed so fond of Wallace.

Chapter Twenty-six

Pete had guessed correctly. Wallace had traveled to the spring by the willow. It was a familiar and comfortable place he knew. He reached it the evening he left the Garbs, and he took a long drink and lay in the water for a while. Then he rooted around among the water grasses and found enough to eat in the darkness, and after that he went to sleep.

In the morning he wandered around eating roots and grass. This place by the spring reminded him of something that had never entirely left his pig mind. When he had first come to the spring, he had been more or less on the way to his own home, and being here again gave him that feeling of wanting to be back where he belonged. He talked to himself about it as he rooted. He seldom said "Oink," but he said "Woink" and "Ernk."

It was a cool, sweet morning. It was not going to be so hot as some of the summer days had been. Again Wallace started to travel in what he felt might be the direction of home, but he had the same trouble that he had before. He grew thirsty and had to return to the spring.

As he approached the water, he stopped and made a surprised sound. There were people there.

Two young men were resting in the shade. They had guns with them. Neither had had to go to work this day, and they were enjoying the summer morning by walking into the hills and killing things. They had shot a few song birds, just for practice. They had killed ground squirrels, which they had no desire to eat, and they had some bloody dead rabbits with them that they planned to take home for their wives to cook.

They both looked up when they heard Wallace.

"I'll be darned. There's a pig," said one.

"Shoot it," said the other.

"Naw. You got to kill a pig properly to get good meat. Wait. Maybe we can catch him. He's got a piece of rope on him."

The frayed end of Wallace's rope hung under his chin like an untidy necktie.

"Come pig, so-o-oey pig."

Feeling a little wary, Wallace stared at them. "Erful," he said.

"Hey, look here, pig." One of the men fished in his pocket and brought out a sandwich wrapped in oiled paper. Wallace smelled the food as the man unwrapped it. He tossed a piece of bread toward Wallace, and Wallace ate it and stepped nearer.

Carefully the man reached out a hand. "Nice piggy, come here."

Wallace saw no reason to run. The man stood up and moved toward him. Wallace started making conversation and wasn't alarmed when the man took hold of his rope and then petted him.

"Say, this is a good pig. Just about right. A fat young barrow."

"How we going to get him home?"

"Easy. We'll just lead him down to the road and load him in the station wagon. I got a pigpen. We'll share the cost of grain feeding him, and then when we kill him, we'll each have half the meat. As soon as it gets cool, in the fall."

"That sounds fair enough."

"Wonder where he came from."

"Maybe he got loose from those hog pens down the road from where we live. They got a lot of spotted pigs there."

"He's got no earmark. They can't prove he's theirs."

"Finders keepers. Well, let's get going."

Wallace was pleased to be with such friendly people. He had a tendency to feel lonely when he wandered by himself. He led with no trouble. Indeed he would have followed whether anyone took hold of his rope or not.

They took a rough trail out of the brushy hills, down to the nearest road, where the men had left their car. They opened a back door. One pulled, one pushed. Wallace stepped into the car, and the door was slammed shut. He rode very well, looking out the window and grunting from time to time.

The children reached the spring shortly after Wallace had left with his new acquaintances.

"Oh, look!" cried Christina happily. "Wallace is around here somewhere. See all the fresh tracks and where he's rooted." She began calling him.

Pete said nothing for a while and then he observed, "People tracks, too. Lookee. And the pig tracks going right with these. Someone's got your pig."

"Oh!" moaned Christina, her hopefulness vanished.

"How awful!" Doreen was all sympathy. "When we almost had him found."

"Maybe they're not too far. Let's hurry and follow the tracks," Kathy suggested.

The tracks were plain to see. And when they got down to the road, it was easy to read what had happened.

Christina wailed, "Someone's put him in a car and driven off."

The children looked at one another in dismay. They couldn't think what to do next.

Chapter Twenty-seven

THE men hadn't far to drive to where they lived. They pulled into the driveway and yelled for their wives and children to come see what they had. Three little boys peered into the station wagon and giggled to see a pig there. The wives expressed dismay. "What did you have to bring home a pig for?"

"Good eating. Wait and see. Now you kids stand back. Don't scare him, and we'll put him in the pen."

"Got any table scraps?" asked one of the men. "Johnny, run and get them. We'll kind of coax the pig along, and he won't try to get away."

When Johnny came with a pan of scraps, Wallace was allowed to smell it, with the door open just a crack. Then, carefully, he was ushered out of the car and led to his new home with the pan just out of reach of his snout.

"Here, let's take that piece of rope off him."

"We better make sure that the pen is good and solid, so's he won't get out."

Wallace ate potato peelings, carrot tops, and banana peelings, but he wouldn't eat orange peelings. While he was eating, the men found a few places to repair in the fence.

The pen had had no tenant since the middle of last winter, and weeds had grown tall. Wallace found tasty things as the men worked on the fence. One of the boys brought him a bucket of water, which he appreciated. So far as anyone could observe, he seemed contented.

The boys hung around after their fathers left and watched the pig. Then, finally, they went off to play.

Wallace worked on the weeds a while longer, then, being sleepy, settled down for a nap. A pepper tree hung shade on one side, which he found comfortable.

When he wakened, he finished the weeds and began to grow lonely and restless. He grumbled and poked at the fence. In a few minutes he had found a weak spot, broken a board, and was out, trotting happily down an alley.

He smelled something delicious and investigated.

In a back yard was a neat vegetable garden. Wallace looked longingly at rows of young corn, at tomatoes and cucumbers and squash. He shoved his nose against a chicken-wire fence.

Fences were now no problem to Wallace. By pushing in the soft dirt, he lifted the fence up and crept under to start enjoying a banquet.

At first no one saw him there. The garden was between the minister's house and the church. Wallace was so whole-heartedly concentrating on what he was doing that, when he was discovered, he was taken by surprise.

The Reverend Mr. Landers stepped out his back door and gazed in horror at what was happening to his garden. "Hey!" he shouted, and ran toward the garden gate. Wallace was so startled that he shrieked and bounced against the fence, but he was too panicked to make a planned escape. Then he saw the gate opened and rushed through it.

The fact that Mr. Landers was standing in the gateway didn't alter Wallace's course.

Wallace pushed between the minister's short legs. The

man sat down upon him, though not willingly. Wallace screamed bloody murder and kept going.

Mr. Landers somehow couldn't manage to fall off at once, and riding backwards, his feet dragging the ground, all he could do was to yell. The swift, brief ride took him past the side of the church and onto the sidewalk of Main Street.

There, seeing people, Wallace suddenly swerved to head back toward the alley and lost his rider.

As he picked himself up, the Reverend Mr. Landers said a few words not ordinarily spoken by ministers—at least not in that manner.

He met the scandalized gaze of several members of his Ladies' Missionary Society, who were about to enter the church for a meeting.

"Goodness' sake! Mr. Landers riding a pig. And *backwards!*"

"And such *language!*"

Unfortunately his misadventure had been witnessed by others, too. "Holy cow!" he heard a loud-voiced man say. "Did you see the preacher riding a pig?"

It was the lowest moment in the young man's life. Fortunately for Wallace, everyone was so stunned with amazement that no one thought to give chase right away. Among the fascinated spectators were his old acquaintances who called themselves Pedro and Pancho. They stood staring stupidly at the embarrassed minister until a thought crossed the mind of Pancho.

"Hey, that looked like our pig. The one we had on the Fourth of July. Which way did he go? Come on, Pedro. Let's get him."

Chapter Twenty-eight

T HE next morning Christina's mother took her in the car, and they drove around town, up and down alleyways, and circled the edges of town, again hoping to see Wallace in someone's yard.

Christina reasoned that the car that had picked him up must belong to someone who lived in or near the small town. He wouldn't have been taken down to the city by the coast because pigs aren't allowed to live in the city.

On the other hand, he might have been taken miles away to some ranch. This didn't seem quite so likely because who else but someone from this town would be walking back in the hills by the spring? Someone who lived miles away wouldn't be going into those hills on a summer morning. He'd have places nearer home for hiking.

Wallace just had to be in or near town. But where?

The unbearable part of it was that they had come so very near to finding him, if only they had gone to the spring earlier yesterday!

" 'If' is such a horrid big word," Christina mourned.

On the way home her mother thought of something. "We should have stopped in at the sheriff's office. They might have heard about a stray pig. Well, you can phone when we get home."

"You phone," said Christina.

"No, it's your pig."

When they reached home, there were Pete, Ginger, and Kathy. "We were just going to ride over to the Garbs' again. He might have gotten loose and headed back that way."

"I'll get Button," Christina said.

"Aren't you going to phone the sheriff?" her mother reminded her.

"What'll I say? I mean how do I say it?"

"For goodness' sake! Just tell him about your lost pig."

"Say that you are phoning to report about a stolen pig," said Kathy.

To Christina's amazement, the man who answered the phone began to laugh when she told about her pig. "There was some incident in town yesterday concerning a pig. It got into the preacher's garden. There was quite a commotion."

"There was? But where is my pig now?"

"I don't know. No one's reported seeing him since."

"Oh, please look for him. I've got to find him."

"Well, we'll do our best."

Christina turned away from the phone in despair. "If only we'd looked for him in town yesterday! He was right there in the preacher's garden."

"We didn't seem to know what to do yesterday after seeing he'd gone off in a car. Of course, that's what we should have done." Ginger sighed unhappily.

"At least he must be in town, or near," reasoned Kathy. "Unless he's gone to Garbs'. And you just looked in town and didn't see him, so let's go on to Garbs'."

"Just driving around town doesn't seem to do much good unless we could stop at every single house and ask."

Christina felt gloomy on the way to Garbs' until she

133

thought about the puppy. It would be a comfort to see him again. In her despair over Wallace, she had forgotten to ask her mother about the puppy, but somehow she felt sure that her mother would let her have him.

Doreen ran to meet them when she saw them coming. "Did you find him?"

"No. We thought maybe he'd come back here."

Doreen shook her head sorrowfully. "I wish he would."

"Well then, he must be somewhere in town, unless he's on the way here."

Mrs. Garb came out of the house. "Did you come after your pup?"

"Not today. We're still looking for Wallace." Christina got off Button and picked up the puppy. "It's a wonder he doesn't get stepped on by some horse." The puppy began wiggling with happiness. He loved being held.

"Did you find out anything at all about the pig?" Mrs. Garb asked.

Christina told her what she had learned, and Mrs. Garb said, "I know what! Mr. Garb has to work all day in town tomorrow, hanging wallpaper in a house. Why don't all you kids come here early? You can put your horses in the corral and then ride into town with Mr. Garb in the truck. You could spend the whole day looking in every single back yard and take your lunches and have a picnic in the park. And when Mr. Garb gets off work, he'll bring you home, maybe with the pig, too."

"Oh, that's great. Let's!" Christina gave the puppy an extra joyful squeeze, and he grunted.

"And even Freddie and Ernie can come," Doreen decided.

Teensa, thinking of store windows and other delights of town, offered to join the search.

But her mother said, "Nope. Somebody's got to stay home and help me. Teensa, you never was interested in that pig."

Teensa looked sulky and went off to comfort herself with a movie magazine.

"Will your mothers let you spend all day in town?" Christina asked.

"I should think so," Kathy said. "This is so important. Yours will, too, won't she?"

"I'm sure she will. It isn't as if I'd be alone. She wouldn't worry with all you along."

Doreen suggested, "Let's all ride down and look around the spring again. He just might of come there."

They found no new trace of Wallace by the spring, but they had a pleasant time because they felt so hopeful about the day in town.

Doreen said, "Funny, now I'm trying to track Piggy. He used to track me."

"Oh, did you play hide and seek with him, too?" Christina asked.

"Yes, I'd sneak off and hide in the bushes and hold real still. And I'd hear him snuffling along, making funny sounds, and then he'd always find me and be so glad. I used to peek out and watch him looking for me. He'd seem real worried."

Kathy laughed. "What fun. I never knew that a pig could be like a puppy."

"Wallace is just wonderful. You'll love him when we find him," Christina promised. "*If* we find him. Oh, dear! He probably must want to find us as much as we want to find him."

Ginger was always hopeful. "I bet we find him pretty soon."

Chapter Twenty-nine

Wallace's one desire after the incident on Main Street was to hide. Looking for cover, he hurried down an alley. He saw where an elderberry dropped over a back fence until its branches touched the ground, and he gratefully crept into a leafy cave. He lay very still as his heart began beating less hard and his breathing returned to normal.

He heard a few cars drive up the alley, and after a while he heard someone walking. Pedro and Pancho were looking for him and discussing the twenty-dollar reward of which Christina had spoken. The nearness of the men reminded him of something pleasant connected with them. He nearly emerged, for he was thirsty. The day was growing hot.

Instinct kept him hidden, however, and the men, deep in their discussion of the glories of twenty dollars, walked on.

Later he heard other people go by. He lay with his front hoofs before him, his head resting on his forelegs, and in that comfortable position he went to sleep.

When he wakened, the day was nearly gone, and he very much wanted a drink of water.

He moved a little and peered out at the alley. It was deserted. The sun was down, and shadows were soothing the scorched earth. It seemed to be a good time in which to go somewhere else.

Wallace didn't quite know in which direction he wanted to travel. He recalled where he had last been served a bucket of water, and finally his hoofs started to carry him toward where that had been.

Presently he smelled dampness and food and pigs. It all interested him, especially the water smell.

His round nostrils told him the way to go, and though he couldn't go directly because of a few houses and back-yard fences in the way, he skirted around and kept to his course. By now it was so nearly dark that he felt safe. He crossed the last deserted street of town, trotted across a vast bare space, and heard pigs grunting and squealing. Sounds and smells were very strong now as he trotted to a board fence.

Inside the fence were many pigs.

Wallace, being afraid of pigs, paused but then felt protected by the fence and hurried along beside it. Somewhere ahead of him was a drink of water. Soon he came to where water had overflowed a drinking trough and formed a puddle, which had spread out under the fence. It wasn't the cleanest of water and it wasn't very cool, but it took care of Wallace's thirst, and then he lay down in it.

After a while he stood up and wandered around, investigating, and found some garbage that had spilled from a truck. This he enjoyed thoroughly and, not knowing where else to go, went back by the water and settled down for the night.

Early in the morning Ezra Sims, who owned the pigs, came with one of his helpers, driving a fresh load of garbage. The pigs, hearing the approaching truck, all began shrieking and running toward the fence.

"Hey," yelled Mr. Sims, a big red-faced man, "there's one got out. Grab him!"

Wallace started to leave immediately, but the men were purposeful and knew how to catch pigs. They knew exactly

at which moment Wallace would dodge and in which direction, and soon one had him by a long ear and one had a hind leg.

"Hey," said the helper, "he ain't ours, or we musta forgot to earmark him."

"Hold him," said Mr. Sims as he pulled out his knife and swiftly cut a slot in Wallace's ear.

Though it didn't hurt very much, he screamed even louder. They picked him up and, to his dismay, dropped him inside the fence on top of shrieking pigs.

The pigs were too intent upon the prospective serving of breakfast to bother about biting Wallace. They were accustomed to meeting strangers as newly bought or newly stolen pigs were cast among them. They were all strangers, anyway. Pigs came, and after a short stay pigs left in a truck bound for market. Friendships, if any, were brief.

These were pigs reduced to the lowest order of pigdom, pigs that had nothing to interest them but the next load of garbage and, between feedings, the hope of finding a comfortable place to rest. There were no trees for shade, only shaded places here and there made of sheets of tin placed on top of posts. The dirty pen was always hot in summer and cold in winter, and sometimes pigs died. Even with such losses, this was a fairly easy way to make money off pigs if enough of them could be ready for market each week. Though top prices were not paid for this kind of pork, the money could keep coming in with very little outlay.

If Wallace had been capable of remembering the pig farm on which he had been born and capable of thinking about it, he would have been astounded at the contrast.

All that he was aware of now was the awfulness of his present situation.

Chapter Thirty

Mr. Garb agreed with his wife. It was a good idea for the children to look for that pig in town. Ordinarily Mr. Garb was a good-natured person. It was only that sometimes he was annoyed at his children and depressed at the inability of the Garb family to get ahead in the world. He seldom stayed annoyed or depressed for long, however, and on this early summer morning he felt cheerful and made remarks about which pretty little girl would ride in the cab with him.

At the very last minute, Teensa appeared, with her hair piled high on her head, wearing the tightest baby-blue stretch pants anyone had ever seen.

"I'm going," Teensa announced firmly. "It isn't right for all these little kids to be turned loose on the town without an older person. And I like that pig. He's not ugly-looking like old Gerber and Hamlet."

Everyone stared at her. Mr. Garb said, "Well, git in, then."

Mrs. Garb shrugged. "I told her she couldn't go. Oh, what's the use? Now, you kids, have you each got a rope in case you find him?"

They all wanted to ride in the truck bed, to feel the breeze and, as soon as they neared town, to have a good view in all directions.

"Quite a truckload," Mr. Garb said when they'd gotten

their ropes and climbed on. "Shall I take them to market, Ma? They might bring a fair price." There were eight of them, all excited and hopeful.

As they approached town, they stared in every direction. Wallace might just be somewhere in view.

Mr. Garb drew up in the driveway of the house in which he was to work. "I think you kids had all better stay together. Safer that way. And when you hear the noon whistle blow, you all come here to the truck and we'll drive over to the park for lunch. Now, don't get into no trouble. Mind your manners and be polite when you ask folks about the pig."

"Yes, Pa," his children said.

Kathy suggested, "First we ought to go to the sheriff's office, just in case he's heard something."

"Oh, Kathy, you come with me," Christina said.

"Don't be so scared of people. I used to be, but I'm not any more. I'll go in with you, though."

The young deputy smiled at the girls. "What can I do for you today?"

"Has anyone seen my pig?" Christina asked anxiously.

"Haven't heard any reports. And I've cruised around and looked, but I haven't seen him. I sure hope you find him soon. He could get into someone's prize flower garden, and your dad might get sued for damages."

"Oh, dear."

"But probably you'll find him all right. And I'll keep an eye open. Let me know if you need any help."

Back on the street again, Kathy said, "I know that Mr. Garb said we should all stay together. But with eight of us going eight different ways, that would make the chance of finding him eight times more."

"That's exactly what I've been thinking," Doreen agreed. "Only Freddie and Ernie better stay together. They're little. I don't trust one of them alone, or even two of them together much."

"That would make seven chances, which is pretty good. Let's."

Pete wanted to know, "But golly, what if someone finds him right away? How'd the others know? They'd keep on looking."

Doreen said that they could all report back to the truck from time to time. "Like every hour or every hour and a half. Even if someone did find him and the others kept hunting, it wouldn't hurt. It'd be so good to find him, and the others would learn pretty soon. Now you're sure you'll know him? Only me and Christina and Freddie and Ernie and Teensa ever seen him."

Kathy interrupted. "I saw him at the show the day he ran away."

"That's right. Well, anyway, remember, he's got fifty-one spots, he's pretty big now, and he's got long going frontwards ears."

"O.K.!"

They all went their various ways, and Doreen hurried to the nearest alley and started traveling west. She peered into all back yards, and from time to time she called, "Here, Piggy, Piggy."

Her westward course brought her to within smelling distance of the commercial hog pen, and she approached it hopefully. It seemed logical that the pig might have gone there.

"Pew!" she said to herself.

The day had turned out to be cooler than the previous

one. A breeze blew from the west and brought the smell of bad garbage right into the fringe of town. "A wonder they stand for it," she thought.

She crossed a side street, hurried over a stretch of bare vacant land, followed the rutted road the garbage trucks used, and stared, hopelessly, at all the dirty pigs. A number of them came running eagerly to the fence. It was difficult to tell about the markings of any of them, they were all so plastered with mud. There were many of the general size of Wallace, with the same type of ears. The ones that had come to the fence started making friendly sounds at her, and she picked up a stick and leaned over to scratch some backs. With one another the pigs were cross and irritable. Some pig was always biting another, and sounds of protest were many.

"Poor things. They got nothing to do and no decent place to lay down. Piggy wouldn't like it here at all, and Gerber and Hamlet just don't know how lucky they are."

As she stared around, she thought, with a tingle of excitement, that she saw Wallace. He was standing dejectedly alone. He looked a little heavier than the others his size, but he was so dirty that he was hard to recognize. Doreen wanted to get a closer look.

She called loudly, to be heard above the sounds of gruntings and shriekings, "Piggy! Come, Piggy!" She was sure that he lifted his head eagerly, but her call brought a large number of others running toward her.

She started walking beside the fence, toward a gate she saw further on. "Wallace! Is that you Wallace? Come, Wallace. Wally, Wally, Wally!"

The pig started gladly toward her, but so did all the others. "If it is him, how'm I gonna get him out the gate?

Wisht I could get a better look. Get back, you pigs, go on now. Wallace, you come here!"

Obviously he wanted to come; obviously there were too many hostile pigs in his way. "If it is him, they sure got him buffaloed. He don't act much like Piggy. But then, Gerber and Hamlet had him buffaloed, too."

She wondered about climbing over the gate, swatting the others with a stick, and being able to get close enough to see for sure if this could be Wallace. She was nearly certain that it was.

The thought of climbing in with such a large number of strange and hungry pigs was a little frightening, and she perched on the gate and tried to decide whether she should or should not.

She had not long to ponder because the owner of the pigs came driving in. "Hey, you kid, what you doing there? Get out."

"You got our pig. I'm trying to get him out the gate."

"I ain't got your pig. Them's all my hogs. You get outta here before you get into trouble."

"Help me get my pig, and I'll go. It's that one over there."

"Ain't yours. See, all my hogs got my earmark on 'em."

"That don't prove nothing. You could have marked him when you put him in."

"Ain't a fresh mark."

"How can I tell? It's all covered with mud."

Doreen was not one to back down easily. The man glared at her. "Now you go."

She stood her ground.

"I'll have you arrested for trespassing."

She retorted, "I'll have you arrested for pig stealing."

"Now listen, little girl, I'm running out of patience. You

know what? I could pick you up and toss you into that there pen, and them hogs would eat you up, hide and bones and everything. No one would know where you was. How'd you like that?" He made such a threatening move toward her that she jumped off the gate and darted out of reach.

"Yah, you wouldn't dare. You just try it!" She ran back and shook the gate desperately. "Wallace, come, Wallace!"

"Get!" yelled the man so ferociously that Doreen fled.

"Anyway," she thought, on the way back through town, "I'll tell my father and the sheriff and everyone, and Christina will know her pig all right, and she and the sheriff could just come and get him and put that man in jail."

Ezra Sims was thinking, "I'll get my helpers, and we'll load that hog and them others that's ready, and we'll haul them off."

If there was some question about ownership, it would save trouble to get that particular one to the packing house right away. Not that a kid would know one hog from another or have any way to prove anything . . .

Chapter Thirty-one

Hearing someone call his own name made Wallace even surer that he did not belong here. He had thought that Doreen was going to let him out, but she had gone, leaving him with a desperate longing for a familiar place and his friends.

He made his way to the gate where he had seen Doreen and snuffled at it, muttering to himself. He pushed against it and tried rooting under it. For a time nothing happened, but Wallace was persistent. Furthermore, he was strong. He braced himself and shoved mightily. It was a firm wooden gate with a good catch on it. He kept pushing, rooting, tearing at it with his teeth, jiggling it. The catch stayed firm, but then a loose screw dropped from a hinge. Then another.

Several pigs crowded around him curiously. One bit at another, and that pig, trying to get away from his assailant, gave the gate a good bump. Suddenly it sagged on one hinge, and that pig went right on through. So did Wallace and a large number of others.

Making pleased grunts, Wallace trotted briskly back toward town. Others went in the same direction. They smelled damp green lawns and the clean turned earth of gardens.

Pete was the first to see a pig. It was covered with dry mud, so that he couldn't tell for sure exactly how it looked, but it was a pig with hanging-forward ears. It was right as to size, and Pete tried to get near it. "Come, Piggy, come, Wallace," but it hurried away. Pete ran after it.

In the sheriff's office the phone began to ring.

"There's a pig on my lawn."

"Oh, good," said the deputy.

"What do you mean, good? That pig's doing damage."

"I'm sorry. I mean some people want to find that pig."

"Come get him, then."

The deputy no sooner hung up than the phone rang again. "There's a stray pig in my flowers. A big one."

"That's funny," said the deputy.

"What's funny about it? Get it out of here."

"Yes ma'am," and he was about to hurry out when the phone summoned him again.

"There are three pigs in my husband's vegetable garden. He isn't home, and I'm afraid of them."

"Yes ma'am, I'll be right over."

The phone started ringing again as he dashed out the door. He didn't stop to answer it. "What's going on, anyway?" he said, puzzled.

He soon saw.

The town was invaded by pigs.

Housewives with brooms were chasing pigs from their lawns to neighboring lawns. Men with sticks were running pigs out of gardens. A panicked pig ran down a sidewalk of Main Street and upset the newspaper rack by the drugstore. Then he bumped into the druggist, who had run out, and upset him also.

The pig started across the street. A car's brakes were jammed on. There was an exciting crash as one bumper hit another.

Several men had caught pigs and were trying to hang onto

them, and it was difficult to tell whether people or pigs were making the most noise.

People yelled, dogs barked, pigs shrieked.

The town had never experienced anything like this.

One smart pig ended up in his own back yard, in his own pen, where he rested gratefully. He had been a stolen pig.

Christina and her friends were stunned by the number of pigs. Doreen jumped up and down. "One of 'em's Wallace, I know. He was over at the pig place. I seen him. Somehow they've all got out."

"I haven't seen him yet," Christina gasped, running beside Kathy. "Oh, I hope nothing happens to him. Someone might start shooting pigs!"

A few wise pigs found a place to hide in shrubbery. Most of the pigs grew tired, for a pig is not constructed to keep running for a long time, especially in summer.

The pig truck came roaring up Main Street. "Got to catch 'em," the owner yelled to his two helpers, and jammed on the brakes. "There's one. Get him!"

It wasn't Wallace.

Not caring for so much violent confusion, Wallace was heading for a place he remembered in an alley. He wanted to creep into his cave, where the elderberry branches hung low.

He was very nearly there when, above all loud sounds, he was sure he heard his name being called. He stopped and listened. He heard it again and was trying to decide whether to go toward that sound or to proceed to his hiding place when he had no choice but to run.

Pancho and Pedro had come wandering down the alley.

"Hey! There's our pig again!" They started after him, and Wallace left immediately.

He charged through a side yard and was dismayed to find himself being chased toward the thick of the confusion. Several people grabbed at him as he dodged this way and that.

He heard Doreen. "There's Wallace! Here, Wallace, here, Piggy!"

Wallace knocked a boy out of his way and, with his last spurt of energy, fled toward the voice.

A man grabbed him and hung on. "I got him. Where's my truck at?"

"Oh no, you don't!" cried Doreen. "That's not your pig!"

"You again!" Mr. Sims was nearly howling with rage. "Get outta my way."

"Christina!" shrieked Doreen. "Here he is! You leave go, Mister. He ain't yours!" She seized one of Wallace's kicking legs and hung on. Wallace still had plenty of screams left in him and was using them.

The man shouted, "Where's the sheriff? This is the kid that probably let all the pigs out. Hey, where's the law?" He reached out with his free hand and grabbed Doreen by her pony tail. Her yells were as loud as Wallace's.

The children came running.

Teensa, who had been enjoying the excitement, rushed at Mr. Sims. "You leave my sister alone! You let go our pig, too!"

"Go away!" he roared.

"You leave my sister be!"

If there had been room for further amazement, Teensa's relatives would have been amazed. She became a wildcat again. She kicked and scratched. Suddenly her sharp white teeth bit the man's wrist.

"Ow!" he yelled, releasing Doreen. "Ow! You little demon!" and he grabbed Teensa's hair. This was a mistake.

"I'll claw your eyes right out!" Teensa shrieked, and it seemed that she would.

Ernie and Freddie, watching breathlessly, felt that it was safe for them to attack and, thankful that their mother had made them wear shoes, started kicking.

"Ow, my shins! You kids scram!"

Pete put out a foot, and the man went down. Teensa was on him, pommeling and yelling with savage delight.

Doreen had Wallace by an ear and a leg. "Help me!" She was on the ground, hanging on with all her might, because of course Wallace was too terrified to recognize a friend. Kathy sprawled across him, and somehow Christina got her rope around his neck, tying knots with trembling fingers. No matter what, he must not escape this time. "Keep hanging on," she urged. "The rope might not hold him."

By now a crowd surrounded them. This was more interesting than chasing pigs from lawn to lawn. The deputy pushed through.

"Now what?"

"Arrest these kids!" gasped Mr. Sims, looking up from his unfortunate position.

"This is my pig," Christina stated firmly.

"It ain't. See, he's got my earmark."

"You probably just put it there," Doreen cried. "Wash off his ear and take a good look."

"Got a bill of sale on this pig?" asked the deputy, pulling Teensa to her feet and helping the man to stand.

"Sure I have," puffed Mr. Sims. "I got him in with a whole bunch I bought over to Green Valley. I'll show you the papers."

"That don't prove nothing," Doreen argued fiercely. "How you gonna prove that this pig was part of that bunch?"

"How you gonna prove he ain't?"

The deputy scratched his head.

Christina found time to think that never was there anyone like Doreen, so quick to know what to say.

"Because," said Doreen, "this pig has fifty-one spots and one ear with a dab on it and one not. His left ear."

"Har! How we gonna count spots on these here pigs, all of 'em runnin' wild after you let 'em out? Lots of these could have that many spots and a one spotted ear. Anyway, look at ears. Look at my earmark. You ought to go to reform school, lettin' all my pigs out."

"I didn't!" Doreen turned to the deputy. "Arrest this man for stealing this pig."

"Well, we can't settle it here," said the deputy. "Guess we'll have to impound this pig and settle it in court later."

"Can't prove a thing," the pig man repeated.

"Oh yes we can, and right now! I know how." Doreen began whispering to Christina.

Chapter Thirty-two

"I'm afraid it won't work," Christina whispered back. "He's too scared. It'll be like the other time."

"Keep your rope on him. And tell the people to keep quiet and not scare him. He ain't so scared any more, anyway."

This was true. Wallace was feeling safer with his friends around him. He had stopped squealing and struggling. He was tired.

Doreen picked up a stick and began scraping at the dried dirt that covered Wallace. "He sure smells," she observed unnecessarily. "I'd like to hug him if he wasn't so dirty. Pet him with a stick."

Christina crouched over him and rubbed him gently. Wallace lifted his dirty snout and said in his old affectionate way, "Ca-ca-ca!"

"Wallace!" cried Christina, happy. "Next you will be saying 'Erful.' "

"Erful," Wallace remarked.

"Well, did you kids get through with your confab?" said the man impatiently. "Because me and this pig's leavin' in a minute unless you can prove somethin' for sure. And you can't."

Doreen whispered to Christina, "Got anything good in your pocket?"

"Oh, yes. I have some lump sugar."

"Let him smell one now, but don't give it to him yet."

This seemed to be the best thing that had come near Wallace's nose since the Fourth of July. He stood up eagerly and pushed at Christina.

Suddenly, to Christina's astonishment, Teensa became a different person. She had been listening to Doreen's whispering.

She stepped forward and bowed low. Her hair had fallen down, and again she was a pretty young girl.

Teensa cleared her throat. "Ladies and gentlemen, may I have your attention? Will you please draw back a little? That means you, too, Mister," she added, eying the pig man sternly. "Now, ladies and gentlemen, with us we have the world-famous trained pig, Wallace the Wonder, who has performed before the crowned heads of Europe. He belongs to Miss Christina Wood, owner and trainer. I must request that until this performance ends you keep as quiet as you can. Don't laugh please, or don't applaud yet. I thank you." She bowed again, first to the audience and then to Christina and Wallace.

Some young men whistled admiringly, but not at the pig. Teensa put on her demure expression.

Fascinated and amused, the people stepped back, making a ring around the children and the pig. They were as quiet as if each one were holding his breath.

Only the pig man muttered a little, but not loudly.

Christina touched Wallace's belly with her stick.

"Down," she commanded.

Obediently Wallace dropped.

"Har," said the man. "What pig won't go down to get its belly scratched?"

"Shut up!" someone hissed.

"Wallace, roll over now."

Grunting with effort, Wallace rolled himself over, exposing, for a second, his dirty belly to the clean sky.

To encourage him, Christina popped a sugar lump into his mouth. "Now, stand up."

Wallace scrambled to his hoofs.

"Sit, please," and she offered more sugar. Wallace sat down like a dog, and his audience giggled softly.

"Shake hands," and Wallace politely offered a filthy front foot.

Someone started to leave.

It was the pig man. He was detained by a citizen who cried, "Hold on there! I know now it was you who stole my pig, because he came home when he got loose with those others."

"He musta stole our pig, too," someone else said accusingly. "He up and vanished a while ago."

"Ours, too," echoed a third voice.

"That pigpen on the edge of town is a smelly disgrace. Whole outfit ought to be run out."

"Yes!"

"No way to keep pigs, anyhow. Dead ones laying around, too."

"Look at this girl's pig. A dirty, smelly hog, and he ain't stupid at all. Pigs is smart, give 'em a chance."

Christina's heart lifted like a song. This, after all, was better than a performance with Wallace gleaming and wearing golden hoofs. This was utterly different from her plans of showing her trained animal, but it was much more important this way.

She couldn't help it. She stooped and hugged her dirty pig.

The deputy thumped her gleefully on the back. "Take your pig home, little girl, and don't let him get away again. He's caused us enough trouble. He's probably the smart one that let all the others out. Don't know how they'll ever get rounded up."

With no intention of doing any particular good, Wallace had indeed provided some good moments for his kind. The chase had slowed while people were watching the performance, and that had given the escaped creatures more time to enjoy a few of the pleasures nature had intended especially for pigs. Delirious with joy, they rooted in the soft earth of gardens and plunged their snouts into the cool wet greenness of lawns. A few of them took to the hills and were never seen again.

As for Wallace, he went home with Christina, and very glad he was to be there, too.